Noah had come for her.

Ruth stepped toward the plane and the man standing near the doorway. She gazed at Noah, at his muscular chest, at his firm lips. The cold, remote look etched across his features signaled that his attitude about her profession hadn't changed.

Sighing, Ruth grabbed the plane's railing and pulled her tired body up the steps. At the top, she held out her hand to his waiting one. "Thanks for coming, Noah. I didn't think anyone would be able to get through in that storm."

Her fingers tingled as they remained connected with his. Without his sunglasses on, Ruth noticed his blue irises deepened to the color of the clearing sky before they darkened like the receding monsoon clouds.

Her need to soothe away his anguish intensified, but somehow she sensed that Noah wouldn't appreciate her attempt.

KIM WATTERS

At twelve years old, Kim fell in love with romance after she borrowed Harlequin Romance from her older sister's bookshelf. An avid reader, she was soon hooked on the happily-ever-after endings. For years she dreamt of writing her own romance novel, but after she graduated from college with a bachelor of science degree in business administration, she moved to Chicago to pursue another dream of working as an actress and model. After six years of hustle and bustle, she left the city for the wide-open spaces of Arizona, bought a home computer and began to write.

Kim calls a small town north of Phoenix home, where she lives with her own hero husband, two wonderful children, two energetic dogs and two high-strung hamsters.

On Wings of Love
Kim Watters

Steeple
Hill®

Published by Steeple Hill Books™

STEEPLE HILL BOOKS

Steeple
Hill®

Recycling programs
for this product may
not exist in your area.

ISBN-13: 978-0-373-87582-5

ON WINGS OF LOVE

www.SteepleHill.com

Printed in U.S.A.

In his heart a man plans his course,
but the Lord determines his steps.
—*Proverbs* 16:9

Acknowledgments

For my sister-in-law Susan Clancy.

Big kudos to my critique partners Carol Webb, Linda Andrews and Kerrie Droban. I couldn't have done it without you wonderful ladies. Thank you.

To my last-minute readers, Karin Roepel and Donna Delgrosso, thanks for the extra sets of eyes.

Thanks to my editor Emily Rodmell who believed in me and my story and made it the best it could be.

And special thanks to the following individuals for their generous assistance:

Tracey Knotts, RN, CPTC

Charity Dycus Hagemeier, RN, BSN, CPTC

Paul (da pilot) Dykhuis

Tim Hermesdorf with Aerocare

Any inaccuracies contained within are the sole responsibility of the author.

Chapter One

In his heart a man plans his course, but the Lord determines his steps.

—*Proverbs* 16:9

Ruth Fontaine dodged another puddle as she scurried toward the small group of people waiting to board the outgoing flight at the Scottsdale airport. Her gaze settled on the unfamiliar airplane parked on the tarmac. She skidded to a halt, dreading the impending flight more than usual. Getting acclimated to new pilots and planes was never easy for her. This plane had to be from the new charter airline contracted by AeroFlight, the company that supplied the Arizona Organ Donor Network with transportation to and from hospitals to retrieve organs.

"Everyone here?" Out of breath, Ruth surveyed her teammates. Besides herself, Dr. Cavanaugh, Nancy Tillman, the first assistant, and two med students were going on the fly out to retrieve the heart.

"Yes. We're it," the first assistant replied. Everyone else was oddly quiet.

In the background, Ruth heard the sound of raised voices coming from the interior of the plane. "Vultures. Every last one of them. I don't want them on my plane."

"Keep your voice down. The medical team should be here any minute." An equally angry voice retorted.

"Just once. No more. And this conversation is far from over."

Then silence.

"Okay then." Raising her eyebrows, Ruth twisted her lips and shrugged her shoulders and looked at the assembled group. "So what are we waiting for? I don't think we'll be getting the red-carpet treatment on this flight. I hope you don't mind."

She grabbed the railing and stomped her foot on the bottom step to signal their arrival. The sun disappeared behind a cloud, and Ruth shivered. Aside from the mid-afternoon monsoon, no more rain had been forecast for the day unless the storm came from inside the plane. Not good morale for the team, but none of them seemed to be bothered with what had just transpired.

As she climbed the stairs, Ruth eyed the two men now standing by the entrance. Both wore matching dark blue polo shirts with their company logo embroidered on the pocket and khaki pants instead of the traditional pilot attire, but even without benefit of overhearing part of their conversation, there was no mistaking the tension between the pilots. She could cut it with one of Dr. Cavanaugh's scalpels.

What the pilots chose to wear or their argument was not her problem as long as they got them to and from their destination safer than she'd managed to get her newly smudged bright red manicured toenails to the airport. At the top of the steps, she smiled and held out her hand to the more welcoming man on the right.

"Hi, I'm the donation coordinator, Ruth Fontaine."

"Hi, Ruth. I'm your copilot, Bradford Westberry. Please call me Brad."

"Pleased to meet you, Brad."

"Likewise, Ruth." The tall, stocky, blond man grinned at her, turning on the charm that would make some women swoon.

Ruth preferred the dark, brooding Heathcliff type, like the dark-haired man to her left who commanded her attention. Her gaze transferred to the other pilot, and her stomach turned over as if it hit some heavy turbulence.

His skin was lightly tanned and his face strong and angular. A five o'clock shadow defined his jawline, while a hint of silver touched the dark hair at his temples. Only a crooked nose and a small scar by his left ear marred what she would consider the perfect face.

"Noah Barton. Your pilot." The man's voice held a trace of disapproval as he tried to tilt the corners of his mouth up into a half smile.

Ruth shook his hand and noticed he didn't extend the invitation to use his first name. She felt a slight tremor all the way to the bottom of her feet despite her sleep-deprived stupor from being up most of the last twenty-four hours. She noticed the pilot's jaw slacken as he pulled the black Foster Grant sunglasses from his face. The sadness she'd heard in his tone also flared in his deep crystal-blue eyes as he stared down at her. Her heartbeat quickened, and some strange unidentified emotion passed between them. Ruth blinked. His bittersweet sorrow disappeared behind a wall of professional indifference.

Disappointment nipped at her nerves and startled her. Her reaction to his sudden lack of interest meant this tentative attraction affected her more than she cared to admit.

Not good when she had a job to do. She had no time to get involved with anyone.

Still, the need to chase away whatever troubled him settled in her heart. Ruth leaned toward him and placed her free hand on top of their clasped ones. The action felt right. As if she were meant to comfort him. "It's nice to meet you, too."

This strange meeting confirmed her growing suspicion that today was not going to be routine no matter what she did. Great. After Noah pulled his hand from hers, she slid the right one inside her lab coat pocket and squeezed the heart-shaped stress ball one of her coworkers had given her as a joke, which actually came in handy when she had to step on an airplane.

She couldn't hold the pilots responsible for her bad day that started with spilling coffee on her new white shirt at a breakfast meeting and getting called to the airport in the middle of her mid-afternoon nail appointment after working all night. No. That was just old Murphy rearing his ugly head again at the most inopportune times.

She stepped aside, allowing the rest of the team to squeeze by and enter the Citation.

"Expecting anyone else?" Noah asked.

"No. This is it. I doubt there'd be much room for more." She trailed her teammates. Ruth eyed the six-seat interior as she stepped inside. The plane was smaller than the one the other charter company flew, but the tan leather seats looked just as comfortable.

"Then I suggest you take a seat and fasten your seat belt if you want to get to San Diego by dinner." A no-nonsense sounding Noah followed behind her.

Surprised at his nearness, Ruth spun around. But as she gazed up at him, she couldn't help but think how different this pilot was from the other ones she'd used. None of them seemed to have any issues flying a medical team around. What was Noah's problem?

Again, not her concern right now. Getting the donor heart from San Diego back here to Arizona was. Doing God's will and saving as many lives as she could topped her list of things to accomplish today.

Noah placed his sunglasses back over his eyes as if blocking her from his view. Then he retrieved a headset and handed it to her. "Here. I'm sure you're familiar with these? This is how I prefer to communicate."

"Thank you. I am." Ruth matched his professionalism and placed the unit around her neck. On the newer planes, the interior noise level resembled that of an airliner, so the things weren't necessary like before, but since Noah would be wearing a headset of his own, this meant they could talk without her having to get up and tap him on the shoulder to get his attention.

While Brad secured the door, she eased her fatigued body into the padded seat across from the doctor so she could relay the information from San Diego Memorial. The seat felt as comfortable as it had looked. She sank into the softness. From this vantage point, though, she had a clear view of Noah's partial profile and the frown hugging his rugged lips as he said something to Brad.

The tension grew again between the two men before the other pilot sat down.

Within seconds, Noah folded himself into his own seat and put his headset on. Ruth still couldn't keep her gaze from him. His inexplicable sorrow called out to her on a gut level she didn't quite understand, and the nurturing person inside her responded to it.

She sighed and tossed her curly, blond hair behind her shoulders. Even though Noah had been cordial, his underlying attitude toward her and her team bothered her. People usually gravitated to her. They didn't treat her like she carried a deadly strain of the flu.

Did he really think she was a vulture? Why?

Instead of focusing on him, she turned her attention to the job she'd held for over two years. The job she loved because it brought life and hope to very sick people.

"Okay, team. I'll fill you in on the specifics when we're airborne." Ruth reached for one of the biohazard bags she'd packed and handed it back one row to Nancy. "Here. In case we hit some turbulence."

The pale-faced first assistant grabbed it and nodded.

Unfamiliar with the two med students, Ruth held up another bag. "Anyone else get airsick?"

"We're fine, Ms. Fontaine," one of them piped up.

After Ruth tucked the bag into the seat's pocket, she settled the headset over her ears. Her fingers played with the stress ball as she watched another commuter plane taxi by the window. She loved her job but hated the flying that came with it. Would there ever come a day when she wouldn't be afraid?

A cold, wet nose and a high-pitched bark jolted her from the scenery. A small white, tan and gray dog, a Yorkshire terrier from the looks of it, nudged his snout underneath her palm.

"Oh. Hello, buddy. Where'd you come from?" She smiled at the impish, almost intelligent-looking face.

"That's Houston. He's one of my copilots. He likes to hide until we're in the air. Houston come." Noah's voice resonated through the headset. He snapped his fingers.

The dog's tail thumped against the carpeted floor. His tongue lopped out on one side as he stared up at her with inquisitive eyes. He licked her hand and whined.

"Come here, boy." A growl accompanied the snapping fingers this time.

She noticed the dog listened probably as well as Noah did.

A giggle erupted from behind her tired lips, and she let her fingers trail through the dog's fur. "Houston, huh? I think you're kind of cute. A dog as a copilot. That's unique. Wanna have a seat?" She patted her lap. It only took a split second for the dog to decide her cushioning was probably more comfortable than the seating arrangements behind the pilot's seat.

Noah's last look before he turned around to face the front curled around her heart. Somehow she suspected Houston was more than just another copilot.

"Suit yourself, dog." With the precision of an accomplished pilot, Noah maneuvered them onto the runway.

Cradling her hands together, Ruth bowed her head, closed her eyes and prayed for the safety of everyone on the plane. Then she prayed for the family of the donor and the recipient, asking the Lord to heal all their hurts and wounds and wrap them in his infinite love. Noah, too.

Once finished, and without disturbing her new lap mate, Ruth reached into her coat pocket and grabbed a piece of gum to chew to relieve the pressure on her eardrums when they took off and ascended into the evening sky. The dog watched her every move and sniffed at her hand.

"Sorry, Houston. No gum for you."

The anticipated surge of adrenaline and fear when the plane rolled forward chased away her fatigue. Matching an organ to a recipient and saving a life always had that affect on her. Tomorrow she'd pay the price, but it was well worth the physical strain to bring hope to another family.

"Houston. Quit begging and come here."

The dog whined again and wedged his nose underneath

her arm. His short muscular body wriggled into a more comfortable position.

Ruth laughed and placed the headset on. "For a dog that flies for a living, you certainly are a coward." *Like me.*

"He's got you fooled. He's a sucker for blondes." Noah's voice crackled in her ears.

So Houston likes blondes. What about you Noah? Somehow that last caramel-flavored coffee drink touched off her sarcastic side instead of giving her the much needed energy boost. Ruth tore her gaze from Noah's broad shoulders and looked out the window.

The dusty desert did little to contrast with the buildings in the distance. An occasional palm tree dotted her vision as the world blurred. The bumpy ride on the runway smoothed out like a clean piece of glass.

A haze painted the blue sky as the plane ascended into the thermals. Instinctively, she clasped the stress ball again. Even with all her flight hours, she still had an insane fear of flying. Today's flight was made worse without their usual pilots behind the controls. But Noah had to be as capable or AeroFlight wouldn't have contracted with his company. This was routine.

She ignored the chattering of the med students sitting behind her. Dr. Cavanaugh flipped through the latest medical journal while Nancy filed her nails. Ruth looked out the window again. Rush hour traffic snaked along the 101 heading east. Unless she had another call, she'd be back in the valley by nine and asleep by ten.

A yawn escaped. Her body fought the effects from last night's coordination along with a full day of meetings and appointments. Now wasn't the time to relax. She had calls to make, an itinerary to keep on top of and a staff to direct. She could chill out later.

"Okay, Houston. Time to work." Her fingers caressed the shaggy fur before she set the dog on the aircraft floor.

A sleep-deprived ache registered behind her right eye. Not even pressure from her thumb deadened the pain. Now that they were airborne and she couldn't cause any problems with communication between the pilot and the control center, Ruth placed the headset around her neck, grabbed the Flight Fone and then dialed the coordinator's number in San Diego.

Noah sank back against the pilot's seat as he leveled off to cruising altitude. His fingers strangled the yoke. He'd love to do the same to Brad's neck. He would deal with him later, out of earshot of his passengers. He wondered how much they'd overheard before they'd made their presence known.

Either way, his partner had no right to sign a contract without informing Noah of what would be required. Brad should have known better than to solicit a company like AeroFlight, whose sole mission was to provide medical transportation, including the retrieval of organs.

Human organs. From a donor. From another casualty of the medical profession. Bile rose in his throat. Maybe he should ask Ruth for one of those biohazard bags she was so fond of.

With the exception of his family and Brad, few in his current life knew of his past. But then again, Noah had come to terms with what happened. He'd moved forward with his life.

Or had he?

The moment he'd seen the curvy blonde gracing the stairs of his aircraft, his stomach took a nosedive and landed near the soles of his feet. He hadn't recovered yet.

Against his better judgment, his gaze froze on the reflection of the woman in the tiny mirror he'd discretely mounted up front. Curly hair tied back in a red ribbon revealed a soft, oval face. Her deep green eyes bracketed by an unknown sorrow intrigued him, or maybe it was the delicate slope of her neck and the fullness of her lips.

Wholesome and innocent. For someone else. Not him.

The woman sitting in the first row wasn't Michelle. His wife had died three years ago and taken his heart with her, but Noah saw the same vulnerability in Ruth that brought out a protective streak he fought to control.

A tightness rivaling a wound rubber band tensed his shoulder and neck muscles. He concentrated on forcing oxygen into his lungs. Passing out behind the controls topped the preflight imaginary checklist of things not to do. He didn't need the FAA breathing down his neck.

It wasn't as if they could afford to be choosy at what jobs became available. A fledgling business didn't have the luxury of saying no—not when they had overhead and payroll and other people depending on them. Guilt threatened to consume the shred of sanity Noah grappled to hold on to.

He forced his thoughts back to flying the plane.

"Thanks for the update. We'll be there shortly." Ruth's melodic voice drifted around him through the headset.

He didn't want to hear it. He didn't want to listen to her words. But his fingers refused to isolate her from his communication.

"Okay, team. Here's what we've got. A seven-year-old male."

Noah's grip tightened. *Don't listen.*

"He was struck by a car while riding his bike."

Sweat broke out underneath Noah's arms and across his

forehead. A chill seared his nerves, and beside him he sensed Brad shifting in the co-pilot's seat.

It's okay. I'm over it.

"Medium build, type O blood."

Jeremy…

Maybe I'm not over it.

Disgust wrapped around all the other emotions struggling to surface. How could the woman sitting behind him be so detached to the situation? That boy lying in a hospital bed was a person, not a turkey to carve up and distribute to the neediest person.

His first thoughts had been right. Vultures. Every one of them. Worse than vultures. They were lower than the scum he'd washed off his shoes each summer night on his granddad's farm.

A disembodied voice from air traffic control crackled in his ears. His attention focused on the preparations needed to land the plane safely even though he'd done it a thousand times before.

"ETA is twenty minutes, people. Please make sure your seat belts are fastened," Noah announced, managing to keep all emotion inside him.

"Thanks, Noah." Ruth's voice surrounded him again, lulling him into a false sense of peace.

As he heard Ruth update the hospital, Noah tilted the nose of the plane down, starting their descent into San Diego. He eased back into his chair and concentrated on relaxing.

He needed a vacation away from a past that wouldn't change no matter how many different scenarios played out in his mind.

Once the plane stopped on the tarmac by the waiting ambulance, Noah unclasped his seat belt and looked at the woman in the seat directly behind him. He couldn't help himself.

She represented everything he hated about the medical community. Yet something about her played on his misguided sense of chivalry. Was it a vulnerability he sensed under her professionalism? Or the fear of flying she so gallantly tried to cover?

He watched her rise from her seat. The gold cross suspended from a thin chain around her neck winked at him. The irony that she wore a cross around her neck mocked him. She had the audacity to worship the God he'd turned his back on years ago. Noah didn't have time for all that religious mumbo jumbo, anyway. It meant nothing. But to her, it obviously meant something.

"Here's the dinner list. We should be back in just over an hour." Ruth said softly, her feminine voice cocooning Noah into a false sense of comfort. He shook his head to dispel the feeling. It was part of his job to provide her crew with food for the ride home. He noticed her hand tremble when she handed him the paper. Their fingers never touched; yet he could almost feel her warmth.

"Okay." Noah willed the underlying current running between them to disappear.

"Mr. Barton? Are you all right?" Ruth's eyebrows drew together again, accentuating the tiny crease between them. Her deep green eyes softened as she gazed at him.

"Fine. And call me Noah," Noah responded, but he was anything but fine.

"We need to get going then, Noah. We'll see you later." Her charm bracelet jangled when she placed her hand on his arm. Her touch magnified just how alone he'd been these last few years. He stared in her eyes. For a heartbeat, neither of them spoke. Her mouth opened as if to say something else. She clamped her lips shut and tilted her head a fraction before a smile emerged. As she stepped away, her light, distracting scent disappeared with her. "Bye."

Noah fisted his hands to keep from reaching out to her as he strode to the entrance of the aircraft and watched Ruth descend the stairs.

"If she interests you that much, why don't you ask her out?" Brad joined him.

"I'm not interested." Noah breathed in a lungful of ocean air laced with the distinct scent of jet fuel.

"Right. Then why do you keep staring at her?"

Okay, so maybe he was a little interested, and it scared him. He hadn't thought of another woman since his wife died, and he didn't plan on starting to even though this one caused a tiny blip on his radar screen. Noah wouldn't risk his heart and put himself through the pain and agony of falling in love again and losing her like he'd lost Michelle.

Brad spoke quietly again. "You have to admit she's appealing in a girl-next-door way."

"Not my type." Noah's gaze betrayed his words as it lingered on the blonde coordinator again. Now he knew how the moths that fluttered around his back porch light felt.

"Then what is?" Brad asked.

"I don't know. Not someone like her." Noah ground out. He forced his fingers to uncurl. Even if the only thing that remained from his fighting days was a crooked nose and a few tiny scars, Noah knew better than to tangle with the taller, heavier and younger Brad again. Still his gaze lingered on the woman jumping inside the white and blue ambulance behind the rest of her team. Her hesitant wave before her blond head and white lab coat disappeared inside sucker punched his gut. Anger wrestled with disgust.

The lights flashed against the metal of the hangar to his right. He couldn't shake the image of a big black bird hovering over the emergency vehicle as the sirens echoed in his ears. He continued to watch until it passed through the gate and out onto the street running parallel to the small airport.

"Let me have the dinner list. I'll go pick it up." Brad grabbed the slip of paper Ruth had given him and took off to find the flight-based operation's courtesy car.

Noah's fingers gripped the strap of Houston's leash when he and the dog descended to the tarmac. A walk in the strip of grass would do both of them good after being cooped up in the plane. It might also release the tension tightening his neck and shoulder muscles.

"Come on, boy, we've got some time to kill." He frowned at his choice of words. "Make that some time to waste."

Not really. As if he hadn't learned that every second was precious and not to be frittered away. All those years flying commercial aircraft had eaten away the hours he could have been spending with his family. Now he had the time, but his family existed only in photographs.

His shoes crushed the grass beneath his sneakers as Houston did his business. Why did his partner agree to this contract? Maybe because Brad had recognized what Noah hadn't. He hadn't come to terms with the death of his wife and son.

Too bad. Noah would face his nightmares by himself, not be forced into it by someone who didn't understand. Tomorrow he'd flip the pilot schedules so he wouldn't be called out to do any more organ recovery fly-outs.

Once the distant siren melted into the hum of early evening traffic, Noah relaxed.

Slightly. They still had to get the team and whatever piece of human anatomy they'd removed back to Phoenix. But for now, it was him and his dog. Noah knelt down and scratched the dog his son had picked out behind his ears. The only thing he had left from his happier days. The days when he was half of a whole. Now he wandered around as one of those left behind.

Houston's body wriggled in delight while the dog licked Noah's hand. The adjustment hadn't been easy for him, either, and every once in a while before they'd moved from the house, Noah caught Houston staring into Jeremy's empty room.

Waiting for a boy who would never come home.

He picked up the dog and held his body close to his chest. The dog's heat permeated the thin cotton of his shirt. The nightmares rose to the surface, clawing their way through layers of protective coating meant to shelter his heart. Noah buried his face into the dog's fur. When would the pain go away? When would he feel normal again?

Enough.

He opened his eyes as the almost full moon peeked over the horizon. A light breeze kicked up some of the litter by the chain link fence. With the onset of dusk, he retreated back inside his airplane. Then he settled back in the seat Ruth had occupied because it gave him quicker access to the front.

Her warmth and scent lingered, creating an unwanted longing for female conversation he'd thought was buried behind three years of bitter emotions. He closed off the tap feeding the thoughts and forced them back to the dry recesses of his brain.

With over an hour before Brad, Ruth and the medical team came back, he decided to rest.

As best he could under the circumstances. Noah closed his eyes and almost immediately fell into that bottomless nightmare that had become a part of him.

"Just sign here, Mr. Barton." A jumble of words wavered before his eyes.

"No!"

"There is nothing else we can do, sir. Your son is brain-dead. But there is something you can." The bright red lipstick worn by the garish woman dressed in hospital garb reminded him of an old Japanese movie. The one dubbed over in English where the lips moved independently of the words.

"You want to carve up my son and dole him out like pineapple slices," Noah spat back. Guilt over not being able to do enough to save his son coursed through him like a jolt of electricity.

"Sign the paper, Noah. It's what Michelle would have wanted." His sister spoke softly and rubbed his back. "You know it's the right thing to do."

The clipboard dangled in front of his vision. The line marked with an X tormented him but not as much as the shame. He'd failed his son. A hand he recognized as his own grabbed the pen and scribbled his name.

"Thank you, Mr. Barton. This will save someone's life."

But what about my life?

Noah jolted awake to find Houston licking the tears from his face.

Chapter Two

"Are you okay, Ruth?" Nancy asked as she strapped herself into the seat in the rear of the ambulance to ride back to the waiting airplane.

"I'm fine. Just a little tired."

Exhaustion seeped into her pores again. Child donors were always the hardest. And not very common, which was why so many sick children died while waiting for organs. A fact she tried to change with each donation she coordinated, but sometimes she felt like a hamster trapped inside one of those wheels getting nowhere fast. There weren't enough organs to go around.

She stared out the tiny window in the back over Nancy's shoulder. No need to let the staff know this particular donation had affected her. She wouldn't fall apart in front of the team that depended on her to be the calm one. The reliable one. Boy, did she have them fooled.

But that wasn't what made her unusually quiet. Her silence stemmed from the glimpse she'd caught of the donor's parents' faces as she passed them in the hallway on the way to surgery. A look her own parents had once worn when they realized one of their children was dead. Grief curled around Ruth's heart and opened the door for memories to flood in, carrying debris and fallout from an earlier time.

She'd hoped and prayed for a miracle for her sister that never came. Sometimes she didn't understand God's ways. But she never questioned His intentions, which was why she followed His calling and dedicated her life to making sure every possible donation was a success.

Digging into her purse, she grabbed two pain relievers and plopped them into her mouth with hopes that they would deaden the pain emerging behind her eye again. The heart Dr. Cavanaugh carried in the cooler was two decades too late to help her twin, but another child would have a second chance at life.

"How about you? How are you holding up?" Ruth asked Nancy. The fatigue lines bracketing the first assistant's mouth mirrored her own. The surgery had gone well once they'd finally had their chance to operate.

"Fine, though things could have gone a little quicker."

"That kidney team sure took their sweet time," one of the med students announced. "I didn't think they'd ever get finished. Why did it take so long?"

With six years' experience as an O.R. nurse before becoming a coordinator, Ruth had been involved in hundreds of operations—many successful, others not. Since the heart was the last organ recovered, her team had to wait almost an hour and a half before they could operate.

Things had gotten tricky during the surgery, too, but Dr. Cavanaugh pulled it off. Ruth's team had not lost an organ yet.

"Sometimes things don't quite go as planned. I'm not familiar with that surgeon, but from his appearance, I'd say he doesn't quite have the experience Dr. Cavanaugh has."

"He sure was good-looking though." The other med student piped in. "Too bad that team was from L.A. and not Phoenix."

Ruth leaned against the padded bench and closed her eyes to the inane conversation swirling around her. She put pressure on her eyelid in hopes of alleviating the pain made worse when she realized she still had to get inside a plane and fly back to Phoenix. Instead of finding relief, she saw a sad Noah Barton staring back at her.

"Ready to fly back, Ruth?" Noah's question sounded more like a sigh once she'd picked up her food from the cardboard box next to the door.

"Yes." Ruth had a feeling this flight wasn't going to be one of the more enjoyable ones with a lively conversation. By the looks of the fatigue written on the faces of her team and the tension that still lingered in the air between the two pilots, she predicted it would be totally silent.

Ruth took the same seat she'd sat in on the flight out. Funny how it wasn't as comfortable as before, or maybe she attributed the feeling to the uneasy atmosphere inside. Or more specifically, the heart inside the cooler that seemed to make the air surrounding Noah even chillier. The atmosphere had definitely degraded since their arrival back from the hospital.

As Noah secured the door, her gaze roamed over his profile. She wondered about his slightly crooked nose. A fight? Or some daredevil childhood stunt? Not that it mattered. She wasn't interested. Her hours were consumed with work or volunteering in the children's wing at the hospital. She didn't have time for romance. Not when there was another life to save or another soul in need of spiritual guidance, though Noah looked like he could use a little advice.

Did he even believe in God?

What was it about the pilot that yanked at her emotions? What about him attracted her? Was it the suppressed need that poured from him like rain off a roof? Or the brokenness he unsuccessfully tried to cover? Would he even welcome her attempt to help him?

Doubtful. Ruth's fingers curled around her carton of fried rice. Enough about Noah. She still had a job to do. She just needed to concentrate. "Okay, team. Everyone set? Nancy, do you have your airsick bag?"

"Got it."

"Anyone else need anything?"

No response. Great. With nothing else to think about until they were airborne, her attention drifted back to the pilot.

She watched Noah's long, lean fingers—sprinkled with a light dusting of dark hair—cradle his headset before he put it on.

She wondered what Noah's hand would feel like in hers. What would it be like to have someone to talk about her day with? The triumphs. The tragedies. The little things that happened that she couldn't wait to share?

Ruth shut her eyes as Noah taxied onto the runway. She hadn't had these thoughts about another man since David. But her ex-boyfriend had taken her heart and squashed it like some unsuspecting bug on the sidewalk more than two years ago. There was no way she'd put herself through that again no matter what.

So why was she suddenly having thoughts of relationships? Of being half of a couple? Of being normal? Her job was her life. The kids where she volunteered needed her. Especially the ones waiting for transplants. But somehow she suspected that Noah needed her as well but would never ask.

She squeezed her stress ball as the plane accelerated, whispered a quick prayer for everyone's safety and prepared for takeoff.

Once they were at cruising altitude, Ruth folded the top of her nearly full take-out carton together. Her hunger had disappeared somewhere between Noah's sad, yet bitter, expression and their not so smooth takeoff. In fact, her stomach was probably still hovering somewhere over San Diego County.

"Not hungry? It's what you ordered." Noah's voice whispered through her headset.

Ruth raised her head in time to see disappointment dart through his blue eyes before his gaze slid to Brad. She didn't miss the flicker of annoyance cross Noah's features before he schooled it behind that mask of indifference again.

"The food's fine. I'm tired, that's all." Ruth sighed. Food was not the subject she wanted to talk about right now, but since the copilot and any of the other passengers could hear their conversation, she remained silent.

Noah turned his attention back to the windscreen. "Take a catnap then."

Underneath the pilot's sparse words, Ruth continued to sense an ache, a loneliness that seemed to consume him from the inside out. She'd picked up on it during their flight out and had grown only more acutely aware of it.

Noah wasn't the only one affected by some unknown force. At the bottom of her peripheral vision, she saw Houston lift his head from his paws as his tail slowly thumped on the carpeting. Her heart went out to both of them.

Shifting her gaze from Houston, Ruth looked out the tiny window. Suspended above the horizon, the almost full moon glowed, bathing the interior of the plane in a surreal splash of white. Too bad her emotions couldn't absorb the peaceful feeling as she thought of Noah's words.

"I'm better off staying awake until I can actually sleep for more than twenty minutes." Ruth's fingers tightened around the container of food.

The seams of the white box threatened to collapse under the pressure, so she forced herself to relax. No need to spill tomorrow's lunch on the only lab coat not in the overflowing pile of dirty clothes in her hamper. As soon as she placed the container by her feet, Ruth pulled out her latest lame attempt at knitting a scarf. Keeping her fingers and mind occupied during flight usually helped, especially on the flights home when most of her work was done.

"Suit yourself."

At his words, she closed her eyes again, but Noah's strong, immobile and anguished face stared back at her. If only she could figure why their presence inside the aircraft caused such tension, then maybe she could bring a smile back to his lips.

Nice move, Barton.

Noah watched Ruth in the tiny mirror again. She sat in the same seat as earlier—the seat directly in front of the older woman, a Nancy something. The one who got airsick. So far so good. He'd been lucky, and up until now, no one had gotten airsick yet on one of his flights. Hopefully the woman wouldn't break his record.

His attention drifted to the seat across the aisle from Ruth where the doctor sat. More specifically, the cooler by the man's black shoes. Maybe Noah would be the first to christen his own plane. What disembodied piece of human anatomy lay packed on ice inside?

"It's a heart." Ruth whispered through the headset as if she'd read his mind. "What else would you like to know?"

"Nothing." Noah refused to vocalize the words he wanted to shout in her direction. *Why do you do what you do? Why can't you leave people alone?* But he'd already said enough.

The less he knew about his passengers, the better off he'd be. He didn't want to know their business, where they'd gone to college or why they'd chosen to wear a certain sweater. Let Brad or the company's other pilot Seth be known as the thoughtful, attentive pilots. Emotions got people into trouble. Emotions made people care.

Noah's fingers tightened around the yoke until the whites of his knuckles gleamed. He didn't care. He wouldn't care. He would never fall in love again and experience the pain of having his heart ripped out of him. So why did his mouth go dry when he inhaled the hint of citrus and vanilla when Ruth was around?

"How soon will we be there?" Ruth's voice intruded on his thoughts, enfolding him in her warmth again. A warmth he didn't want to feel.

"About nine-thirty," Noah growled. He couldn't help it. Ruth Fontaine brought out the kind of behavior best left in the boxing ring of his youth. He'd been kidding himself to think he'd been over the deaths of Michelle and Jeremy. The vultures sitting behind him served as a constant reminder of his experience in the hospital. Different people with the same intention. He squeezed the bridge of his nose in an attempt to keep the nightmares from taking control during his waking hours.

"Thanks." Her voice caused a spot of light but not enough to make him change his mind about her.

He still believed the doctors hadn't done enough to save Jeremy because they wanted his organs. Noah would never forgive them for that.

After he heard Ruth update the hospital in Phoenix about their pending arrival, he glanced back again and noticed the knitting project and a ball of yarn she'd pulled out earlier rested in her lap but that the long needles in her hands remained motionless. Houston, his dog, curled up in the aisle by Ruth's feet.

Traitor.

As if she sensed Noah's gaze, her head tilted up. Her green eyes widened over the dark circles underneath them. "Did you need something?"

"No. Make sure your seat belts are fastened, folks. We'll be there shortly." After twisting around to face the front of the plane again his fingers tightened on the yoke. He needed something, all right. But Ruth Fontaine wasn't the answer. He wanted the pain to go away. He wanted the clock to spin back three years so he could relive that last day with Jeremy and Michelle and keep them from riding their bikes to the grocery store.

He wanted his old life back.

But most of all, he wanted to know why the God he'd loved with all his heart had forsaken him and left him to wander alone and troubled.

Relief filled Ruth when the wheels of the plane touched the tarmac. After placing her knitting in her duffel bag, she bowed her head and clutched her hands together, her lips forming the prayer she always whispered once they were on the ground. *Thank you, Lord, for our safe return. Please guide the surgeon's hand in placing the organ You made available to us and grant the recipient a speedy recovery. Your will be done. Amen.*

Her job was done for tonight. Once the ambulance carried the heart and her teammates away, Ruth hitched her duffel bag on her shoulder and turned to face the pilots. "Thanks for the ride. I'll see you around."

"My pleasure. Good night," Brad responded and waved.

Noah cracked a smile that didn't reach his eyes. "Would you like me to walk you to your car?"

"No, thanks. I'll be fine," Ruth said, and before she had a chance to change her mind, Noah turned around and started writing in some type of log.

Fatigue followed her down the steps, across the tarmac and into the dimly lit parking lot where she spied her white Accord parked on the far end. Something didn't look right. Unease scraped her spine and her body protested the pace. She should have taken Noah up on his offer to escort her to her car even if she'd had to wait a few minutes for him to finish his work. She quickly disabled the alarm, unlocked and opened the door and then slipped inside.

She hadn't driven more than a few yards when the thumping noise started and the steering wheel tugged beneath her hands. Now she knew why her car had looked odd. "Great. Just great. Not now, God. Please. Not now."

Her grip tightened. Since she could never fall asleep right away after a donation, a cup of tea, a bath and some Ben & Jerry's were on the agenda for the rest of her evening, not a flat tire.

She pulled the car into the empty space beside a white truck, put it in park and stepped out. Walking around her car, she spied the problem. The right rear tire was flat. She kicked it and winced. Ouch. Now her toe throbbed. Next time she'd do better to remember to wear steel-toed shoes when taking out her frustration on a hard, inanimate object.

With help from the overhead light in the parking lot, Ruth rummaged through her purse. She pulled out yesterday's gas receipt, a pen and then a card from her wallet and dialed her emergency car service. The not-so-distant wail of an emergency vehicle competed with a landing plane as she explained her situation.

"An hour? You've got to be kidding me." She rolled her eyes. Their promptness left a lot to be desired as the bored voice on the other end droned away with some excuse. "Yes, I understand. I know it's late."

Ruth disconnected.

She glanced at her watch. Ten o'clock. Being stranded in an almost deserted parking lot at night made her more than a bit uneasy. A million butterflies took flight in her stomach. Especially when she heard the echo of footsteps approaching. She might just have to attempt to change the tire herself in a minute.

Ruth positioned her car keys in her hand to use them as a weapon if needed. Right. As if a small piece of metal could do much damage. The thought of taking one of the self-defense classes at the YMCA she belonged to struck her as a good idea. Jumping back inside her car, she locked the doors and waited for whoever caused those footsteps to go away.

Suddenly, two familiar figures emerged from the darkness. Ruth's grip on her keys relaxed as Noah's agitated gait and Houston's boundless energy brought them to the vehicle next to hers. She watched Noah pause, take a few steps around the back of her car and then disappear. Houston barked. A few seconds later, she saw the pilot stand up and approach the driver side door, his dog at his heels.

With a forced smile, Ruth flipped on the ignition key and rolled down her window. Too bad she hadn't pulled into the spot next to Brad's car, wherever that was. No. Her knight in tarnished armor had to be the man least happy to see her. "Flat tire."

"I see." His lips formed a straight line.

"Don't worry. The situation's under control." Ruth's words held more conviction than she actually felt. She'd never changed a tire in her life, but that didn't mean she wasn't capable of doing it. She'd just never had the opportunity. She could probably have it fixed by the time the other help arrived.

"Please pop the trunk, and I'll change it for you."

"That's not necessary. I've got it covered."

Noah scraped a hand through his hair and stared at her.

"Look, Ruth. It's late. Your car is disabled. I want to go home, but my conscience won't allow me to leave you here stranded in the middle of the airport parking lot, which if you haven't noticed is not exactly teeming with life right now."

Ruth thought about her options. Wait in the dark for the tow truck to arrive, do it herself or let the handsome pilot wrapped in a blanket of sorrow put her spare on.

The pint of ice cream in her freezer called to her. Banana ice cream, fudge and walnuts just waiting to pass her lips and caress her taste buds. Fine. Ruth would watch Noah change it so she'd know how to do it next time.

"Oh, all right." She popped the trunk and stepped out of the car. Noah had to be able to find the spare tire first. Her body protested the sudden movement as she strode to the rear and an incredulous looking Noah.

"What is all this?" Noah struggled with a large, blue duffel bag.

Out of habit, Ruth reached in and grabbed a business card from the side pocket and handed it to him before she hoisted the second bag out of the trunk. "CPR mannequins. I teach CPR classes on the side. I taught a class on Wednesday and forgot to take them out."

Noah fumbled with the bag and dropped it, just missing his toes and his dog. He couldn't have been more surprised than if the woman had said body parts. Death. Life. What a contradiction. An oxymoron. He stared at the blonde, trying to figure out how such two different people could reside in the same body. Only confusion racked his brain. Shaking his head cleared his mind of his thoughts, but the image of her wide, green eyes remained. So did her signature scent. So why did he tuck her card in his pocket instead of handing it back?

"The heat can't be good for them." Stepping away, Noah opened his tailgate to put the bags on in order to keep the bottoms clean. When he set his down, the contents hit the metal with a thud. No response. Ruth lugged the second one and set it down next to the first.

With the trunk now empty, he rolled back the carpet, exposing what he hoped was a useful spare and the tire iron. He handed her the L-shaped tool, then he tested the spare tire, glad to see it still held air.

"I have a blanket in the backseat of my truck. Could you get it out please?" Noah unscrewed the metal tab.

"Sure."

He felt her gaze on his back as he wedged a rock behind her other rear tire to keep the car from moving while he jacked it up. A bead of sweat trailed down his cheek as he loosened the lug nuts in the dim light cast by the moon and overhead light fixture. After he unscrewed them, he placed them in the exact position from where he'd taken them from her tire. Probably a little fastidious on his part, but he firmly believed each nut belonged to each individual screw.

Just as man and woman were created for each other.

But his other half had died and nobody could take her place.

As Ruth called the car service to cancel her request, Noah worked off his anger on the tire and let it dissipate in the stifling silence around them. He threw the useless piece of rubber into the well vacated by the spare, the loud thunk breaking the silence.

The sooner he changed her tire, the sooner he could slip back into the life of limbo he'd been living for the past three years and forget the memories the woman dredged up.

Now that they were alone, Ruth decided to speak up. She coordinated entire teams during the donation process, so she could handle Noah. Before she changed her mind, she tapped him on the shoulder as he put the spare tire on.

His unguarded expression of sadness and hurt when he turned to acknowledge her made her heart flip. She clenched her damp hand around the stress ball inside her pocket again to keep from reaching out to comfort him.

"Yes?" His gaze roved over her features before a tiny smile split his solemn expression.

Her mouth opened but no words tumbled out. She clamped it shut. Heat crept to her cheeks again, and from experience, she knew they were as red as the blouse she wore underneath her lab coat. Her blushing had always proved to be a challenge—and the brunt of a lot of jokes from her colleagues. As if being a blonde and slightly overweight wasn't enough. What she wouldn't give for a whole garden full of weeds right now to take out her frustration.

"You wanted to say something?" Noah replaced the lug nuts and lowered the car back to the ground before he tightened them.

Ruth composed herself and straightened her shoulders. "I'm curious. Why do you think my team and I are vultures?"

"I was hoping you hadn't heard that." Noah stood and put her jack away before he dusted his hands.

"Well, I did. Care to clarify that comment?"

His unforgiving laughter skittered across her skin, raising goose bumps as he stood and threw the rock that he'd used to keep the car from rolling toward the chain link fence. "Not really. Let's just say I don't care for what you or your team of medical professionals do for a living."

Ruth's attention froze on Noah again, who now stood a few feet from her. The bleak expression carved into his face tugged at the thin string that seemed to connect them together at a subconscious level.

She shuddered as cold seeped into her pores. The overhead parking lot light cast his face into a series of shadows. She stepped back and bumped into the hard metal of the passenger side door. Noah's words confirmed what she'd already suspected when she'd overheard their conversation. David had hated her job, too. At the time they were dating, Ruth had worked as an E.R. nurse and had just started to volunteer with the children. The irony that David worked in medical sales yet couldn't handle not being the center of Ruth's world was not lost on her.

After David's defection and the death of another child she'd grown close to in the Children's Center, she used the opportunity to become a coordinator and lessen the incompleteness she felt.

"My job brings hope and life to people who desperately need it." As an agent of life, she stood on the Lord's side to help others in need. Especially to those who'd drawn the short end of the stick when it came to functioning organs. Like her sister Rachel. Passion filled her voice. "Why can't you see that?

"You and *your* God represent death." His whisper sliced open her emotions and exposed them like raw, open wounds.

Ruth didn't have to guess at his spirituality anymore. What had happened in his life to cause such a rift between Noah and God? She swallowed and fingered the child's butterfly charm bracelet around her wrist. The smooth metal soothed her. The gift that child, Bonnie, had given her before she died before a suitable organ could be found was all the reminder she needed.

No semi-stranger, no matter what his affect on her, was going to tell her any differently. "I'm sorry you feel that way. Thanks for changing my tire. I'll see you around."

Chapter Three

"**R**uth, wait." Noah stopped her. The warmth of her skin under his palm shook his equilibrium. How long had it been since he'd touched a woman outside of a simple handshake?

Before the all-merciful God Noah used to worship took Michelle and Jeremy away from him; that's when. Noah hadn't understood why then, and he still didn't understand why now. And when Noah had needed Him the most, God seemed to have taken a vacation and left him alone to deal with the emptiness and the loneliness.

Ruth placed her hand on top of his in comfort. That one touch, as if she understood him and the conflict warring inside him, undid the bands constraining his emotions. His heartbeat kicked into high gear the same time he noticed she wore no rings. Not that that meant anything. She could have a boyfriend.

"How old is this spare?" Noah continued moments later, thrusting his other thoughts back into the dark recesses of his mind. He glanced at his watch. Twenty after ten. Good thing he'd decided to tape his regular late night shows since seeing them at their regularly scheduled time wasn't an option anymore.

"Five years. Probably as old as the car. Why?" Ruth drew her eyebrows together.

"It may not get you home, and you look ready to drop. How far away do you live?" Noah wrestled with his conscience and scraped a hand through his hair. If her spare blew, she'd be stranded along the road. Not an option. Even in the dim light filtering down from the streetlamp, he could see the fatigue shadowing the delicate skin under her eyes.

"About ten miles from here. How do you know I may not get home? I see people drive around with these all the time."

"Experience. I'll follow you." Michelle had had a similar incidence occur early in their marriage. Plus Noah's mother would have his hide if she found out he let Ruth drive home without making sure she made it safely.

"That's really not necessary."

"It is. I'll be right behind you. Don't take the freeway or drive over forty-five miles an hour. And here. My cell is listed on my card in case you have any other problems."

Ruth bristled but accepted Noah's business card. His attitude reminded her of her older brothers. Which, in the stillness of the late evening, might not be such a bad thing after all.

Weariness bit into her body as she drove home, making sure to follow Noah's advice. If her spare blew, she'd have no transportation at all, and she didn't want to rely on his services again. She couldn't wait for a nice, long hot bath and that pint of ice cream to soothe her muscles. If only it would do something to soothe her mind. The pain written in Noah's eyes followed her all the way from the parking lot like the real Noah did in his white truck. There, but not there.

On autopilot, she turned down the darkened street illuminated by overhead streetlights where her small three-bedroom house sat at the end of the cul-de-sac. The one-story slump block house in an older area of Scottsdale was too big for just herself, but something about it had fulfilled a need inside her.

Her headlights caught the neighbor's black and white cat as it ran across the street and on to her front porch. Great. Why couldn't the cat find another place to hide? Like under her other neighbor's Camaro that he always left parked in front of her house.

Stifling a yawn, she pushed the garage door opener. As she waited, she stared at the tiny porch almost hidden by the overgrown fuchsia bougainvilleas planted on either side. Tomorrow she'd do a much-needed trim session on all her plants and trees and try to work off the feelings brought to the surface by Noah Barton.

By doing something productive, she could retain some semblance of order. Unlike Noah's attitude, her sister's death or all the sick children in the hospital waiting for her to bring them a transplant, Ruth had the power to control her yard, her laundry and even her emotions.

Somewhat. She'd forgotten to finish the laundry she'd started the other day. Before she pulled into her garage, she opened her window, mouthed a thank-you and waved goodbye. Noah's headlights flashed across the exterior of her house as he slowly rounded the cul-de-sac before driving away.

Once inside the kitchen, she flipped on the lights, dropped her bag on the table, placed her uneaten dinner in the refrigerator and then scooped up the mail she'd overlooked yesterday. Then she headed for the phone. She'd been gone all day. Even a friendly sales call message would be welcome right about now.

The quiet didn't usually bother her, but with the memories of Rachel and Bonnie hovering near the surface, the stillness brought home the fact that something was missing out of her life. Burying the need for a companion with work and volunteering wasn't working as well as it had before. Her "one day" had changed to "today." She wanted a partner. A husband. A child or two to cuddle. She wanted someone to hang out with after work. Someone to talk over her day with. Someone to commiserate with.

God was there for her and always would be, but suddenly she wanted more than a one-sided conversation. Ruth bowed her head in shame. So what if the Lord didn't talk back to her in words. She felt His comfort and His love all the time. He would never forsake her or fail her like others around her had.

Feeling better, she flipped her hair into a knot at the base of her neck, wandered into her dark kitchen and flipped the light switch. She thought about Noah.

Another Mr. Wrong.

Ruth grasped the freezer door and pulled. Much to her disappointment, only some waffles, a bag of frozen peas and a few ice trays resided inside. She wrinkled her nose when she realized she'd eaten her last pint a few nights ago. After smacking the door shut with her hip, she filled the teakettle with water and turned on the gas burner.

Her thoughts wandered to Noah again as she keyed her way to her voice mail. Unlike David, at least Noah didn't lie or misrepresent himself about his beliefs. Even until the end, Ruth had believed David had been as committed to the Lord as her until she found out differently.

Five minutes and seven messages later, Ruth kicked off her shoes and pulled her feet underneath her as she sat on her oversized toffee-colored couch. The cup of tea she'd brewed sat on the distressed hardwood coffee table. Her gaze scanned the contents of her mail—bills, what looked like an invitation and a few credit card solicitations.

Her hand stilled on the society magazine she kept forgetting to cancel. Out of habit, she glanced through pictures of the "Who's Who?" of Phoenix. A strangled cry escaped her lips as she stared at the picture of David with his new bride.

Betrayal stabbed her. Ruth squeezed her eyes shut and blindly reached for her cordless phone. Obviously David had no problem committing to another woman; it was just Ruth he had a problem with.

Tilting her head back to rest against the cool leather, she dialed her older sister's number and waited. Karen had always had a knack of knowing when one of her siblings needed to talk. Tonight was no exception as Ruth returned her sister's call. A night owl herself, Ruth knew her sister wouldn't mind the late hour talk.

"Hi, Ruth, you're up late. Work? Or are you seeing someone new?" Her sister's chipper voice carried through the line, reminding Ruth of an earlier time and place. Back in the family fold. Safe and secure without a care in the world.

"David's married." Ruth paced to the laundry room and pulled out the wrinkled whites.

The pause on the other end of the line fed into the insecurities that had resurfaced today. Ruth wrapped strands of hair around her forefinger as her teeth bit her bottom lip.

"Good riddance." Karen seethed.

"What?" Ruth pulled the phone from her ear and let

Karen rant. Her sister's anger surprised her. Of all her siblings, Karen was the most even-tempered of the bunch.

"I never liked him. And how he treated you—"

Instead of shifting the dank smelling, damp clothes from the washer into the dryer, Ruth decided to rewash them as she tried to pacify her suddenly fiery sister. "Karen, stop. I'm sorry I upset you. Forget I mentioned it."

Her sister ignored her words. "What's his phone number again? I'm gonna give him a piece of my mind."

"That's not necessary." The gnawing in Ruth's stomach intensified as she twisted the knob into position and pulled it out to start the cycle. Then she dragged the basket of whites she'd pulled from the dryer back to the living room.

She stared at the picture of her and her two brothers and two remaining sisters sitting on the fireplace mantel. Tall, dark and thin, Karen resembled their father more than their mother, who Ruth favored, with her fuller figure and blond hair.

As usual, Ruth was stuck in the middle. The same as her birth order. But that wasn't the reason for her position in the picture. Her siblings crowded her to protect her as they hadn't been able to protect Rachel. "I can fight my own battles now."

Her sister protested. "But it's something we've always done."

Ruth's fingers tightened on the phone. It only took a phone call to undo the progress she made over the years away from her family. "I know, and I appreciate it. But I'm not a baby anymore. And I'm not going to die like Rachel."

The silence drained her further.

"Listen. Please don't say anything to the family about

David, okay? I'm over it. He has a right to start a new life just as I have."

Her sister's sudden lack of words freaked Ruth out, and if she'd had any energy left, she'd be pacing the room.

"Right. I love you and I just want you to know that I'll always be there for you. No matter what. Call me anytime. Day or night." Karen's soft voice reached out through the telephone.

"Thanks, Karen."

"Now to get back to my question. Were you working or are you seeing someone new?"

Ruth dropped back down on the sofa. "Work. "

"You work too hard. Check out that single's group at the church you told me about. Live a little. Have some fun. The best thing for you to do is to start seeing someone else."

"Work is my life. You know that, but if it makes you feel better, I'll see what activities are scheduled for next month." But she knew she was only saying those words to pacify her sister. Still, her voice hitched as an image of Noah Barton appeared in her mind's eye. Heat crept to her cheeks at the thought of the pilot.

The man was all wrong for her. A wounded hero with tons of baggage like herself. Yet she couldn't ignore his anguish and pain. Her nurturing side instinctively took over, and despite the fact the pilot didn't like her career, Ruth found herself wanting to help him.

Her fingers grabbed the colorful striped pillow, and she clutched it to her chest. A stuffed piece of fabric was a far cry from holding another human being in her arms.

"Look, it's late and I'm tired, Karen. I'll talk to you soon, okay? Bye."

After hanging up the phone, Ruth plumped the pillow

and set it back down on the sofa. Then she picked up her tea. She took a sip and stared at the haphazard stack of magazines under her coffee table. The pile of laundry waiting to be folded mocked her. The basket of yarn with two needles poking out screamed amateur over her lame attempt to knit a scarf for her niece. Her life and job had descended into chaos. Starting tomorrow Ruth would get everything organized and tidy, but right now she needed some sleep.

"Hi, Ruth. Glad to see you today." Mrs. Olson, the elderly woman who usually volunteered every weekday afternoon until eight at the reception desk in the Children's Center in the Agnes P. Kingfisher Memorial Hospital in central Scottsdale, pushed the visitor registration clipboard across the counter.

"Hi, Mrs. Olson, what are you doing here today? Where's Margaret Ann? I thought she was due back this week?" Ruth signed her name and grabbed a visitor badge from the basket next to the vase filled with silk flowers.

Concern etched into the retired nurse's numerous wrinkles. "She's come down with a staph infection from her hip replacement surgery. Keep her in your prayers for a speedy recovery."

Disquiet settled across Ruth before she shook it off. The other elderly volunteer was probably healthier than she was. Margaret Ann would be okay, but Ruth would put out a prayer request nonetheless. "I certainly will. So how's my favorite patient doing?"

"Little Marissa's been asking for you all day." Mrs. Olson pulled her reading glasses from her nose and let them hang from the brightly beaded holder. Her faded blue eyes softened and filled with moisture. "Some days are better than others. Today is one of the good ones. I know she and the rest of the kids will be happy to see you."

Ruth's stomach relaxed as she pinned the badge to her blouse. Her gaze skimmed the scenic photos that lined the walls of the foyer and the potted plants stationed by the door. Today they brought a measure of comfort. Five-year-old Marissa was declining rapidly while waiting for a new heart. Each day she remained on Earth was a blessing to her parents, and the staff, and to the lives of the people Marissa touched. "That's terrific. She wasn't doing so well when I saw her on Wednesday."

"Things have changed."

"Thanks, Mrs. Olson. She'll be my first stop then." Ruth stepped away from the counter and headed toward the elevator that would take her to the fourth floor. The elevator bell dinged and the doors slid open. With a final wave and smile to the woman now talking on the phone, Ruth stepped into it.

A few minutes later, the soothing light blue colored walls greeted Ruth as she walked down the hallway toward the playroom where the head nurse had told her most of the kids were waiting—Marissa included. The heels of her sandals clicked an odd beat against the linoleum floor.

Outside room 401 she saw an empty wheelchair. Poking her head through the darkened threshold, she spied the carefully made bed and the unadorned walls and missing trophies and photo frames. A smile lit her lips. The doctors had finally released Johnny Trueblood.

Continuing down the hallway, she saw a towheaded child poke her head back inside the large room at the end of the hall, and soon the sound of giggles erupted the stillness. No chance of making a surprise entrance tonight.

Ruth breathed in the underlying smell of antiseptic and the silent urgency of the staff. They did their best along with the patient's families to let the children lead as normal of a life as possible while in the hospital, but they only had so much time, which is where the network of volunteers was so essential. Not that Ruth minded one bit. She loved her time with the children whether it was reading books to the younger patients, playing games with the older ones or even helping with homework.

She stepped through the door of the room that took up the entire north side of the building and onto the dark, green carpeting meant to resemble grass that complemented the continuous park scene painted on the walls.

Ruth found herself engulfed in the arms of those children able to walk. Others sat in wheelchairs by the big windows, grins on their faces and love shining from their eyes. She couldn't imagine being anywhere else today. Not when she had a roomful of children who needed her and fulfilled her. Her gaze strayed to the little girl wearing a bright pink bandanna over her patchy hair. "Hi, Marissa. I hear you're feeling better today. I'm so glad."

"Yep." The olive-skinned girl gave Ruth one of her sunny smiles. "Did you find me a new heart yet?"

Ruth's smile dimmed. She knew better than to raise false hopes in Marissa or the few others waiting for a transplant. Not that every child here was. Some had cancer; others were recovering from accidents and two had transferred from the burn unit, but those who were waiting or recovering were her favorites. She just wished she could do more to help them.

"Not yet, sweetie, but I'm still looking. It has to be perfect. Just like you." Ruth tweaked the girl's nose.

"Can I sit on your lap tonight then?"

"Sure thing. As long as you share *blankie* with me."

"Hi, Ruth. Back again so soon?" Edina Murphy rocked her sleeping granddaughter in her arms.

"Yep. Nothing can keep me away from my little angels." Ruth tousled Carlos Ramirez's soft, dark brown hair as he held onto her leg.

"Go pick out your favorite stuffed animal and meet me by the reading chair, sweetie. Everyone else, too." Ruth bent down and pried off Carlos' arms from around her leg.

The woman tsked. "It's Saturday night. You should be out having fun, meeting a special man and having kids of your own."

"Now, I thought we'd discussed this before, Edina. I don't have time for a special man in my life right now. I have my work and my kids here," Ruth replied as she walked over to the big bookshelves that dominated the far wall next to the small computer area.

Her thoughts continued to drift back to Noah Barton as her fingers pulled a few children's books from the small kids section.

"Well, you're sure not going to meet him here, that's for sure, unless I can convince my handsome neighbor to come visit, but his schedule is as crazy as yours. I don't know what is with you kids today."

"When the good Lord is willing, I'll meet that special someone. But until then, I've got everything I need right here." Ruth sank down into the big, comfortable mauve chair and kicked off her sandals. Then she patted her lap for Marissa to join her.

Once the bony little girl with her pink blanket, Carlos and the other kids settled, Ruth opened Marissa's favorite book about a village girl and a beast and how love transformed them.

But it was just a fairy tale. Ruth didn't fully buy into the "happily ever after."

* * *

In the office early Monday afternoon, Noah tipped back on the back legs of his chair. He stared at Brad, with whom he shared the cramped room, sitting at the next desk over. "I'm taking myself off rotation for the Aero-Flight calls."

Noah tilted the bottle of soda he'd grabbed from the supply refrigerator to his lips and drank. Above him, muted fluorescent bulbs cast cool light across Brad's features.

"You can't."

"Watch me." Noah refused to go on another organ recovery mission. Let Brad or Seth take it. He didn't need any more memories brought about by ferrying a bunch of medical personnel around. Especially one Ruth Fontaine, who had worked her way under his skin like a sliver.

Brad stared at him long and hard as he played with the pen in his fingers. "We need the AeroFlight contract and about five others to keep us in business. I can't do it all myself. That's not what we agreed to."

"But I didn't sign that contract. You did."

Brad threw the pen across his desk. When he stood, his chair crashed into the off-white wall, the sound reverberating in Noah's skull. "You've been the one nagging about business. I go out and get a decent contract and now you're complaining."

Houston jumped up from underneath Noah's feet, skittered around the desk and cowered behind their office manager, Hannah Stevenson, who now stood in the doorway. He and Brad counted on her to run an efficient office, and she in turn counted on them to keep a roof over her and her young son's head.

"Are you guys okay in here?" The pale, delicate-looking redhead asked.

"We're fine. Just discussing a little business," Brad responded. "How are you doing today? You look nice."

Noah noticed his office manager blushed easily like another woman he'd recently met. A woman who had no reason to intrude on his thoughts today.

Hannah's eyebrows skimmed her bangs as her lips twisted into a hesitant smile. "I'm fine, thank you. Okay then. If you need anything, you know where to find me."

Once Hannah retreated to the front room, Noah pinched the bridge of his nose to keep the nightmare at bay. "But why AeroFlight? Why did you have to contract with them?"

Brad walked over and clasped Noah's arm. "It kills me to see you like this. You think you're living, but you're not. I've watched you suffer for three years. Please. Let Michelle and Jeremy rest. AeroFlight is a wonderful organization and provides a necessary service."

Noah drew back. Raw anger threatened to crush the last piece of sanity he'd struggled to hold on to. He wasn't sure he would ever be able to forgive Brad. "You sound like Ruth."

"Try and see the positive for once." Brad continued.

"What positive? You've been my friend for fifteen years. You were my best man. You were there when Jeremy was born. You met me at the hospital when they brought Michelle and Jeremy in after the accident. You helped with the funeral arrangements."

A tear slipped down Noah's cheek.

His tight fisted hand pushed it away.

"What positive, Westberry? Answer me."

"Your son's organs saved other lives that day. Michelle's could have, too, if she'd been an eligible donor. But you've been too wrapped up in the guilt and denial to see past that crooked nose on your face. Maybe I should break it again." Brad drew back and flexed his fingers.

"Touch me and this partnership is over," Noah growled. "The doctors I counted on to save Jeremy's life created a donor so that someone like Ruth Fontaine could harvest his organs and offer them to the highest bidder."

Brad shook his head, concern etched across his face. His harsh voice pushed through Noah's thoughts. "You don't know what you're talking about. The doctors did everything they could. If you want to blame someone, blame the drunk who hit them. If you don't take the call when it comes in from AeroFlight, we may as well dissolve the business and go our separate ways."

Noah downed the remaining soda and wiped the back of his hand across his mouth. He watched his friend leave to go flirt with Hannah. Brad didn't understand.

Sure, Michelle had been his cousin and Brad had introduced them, but his partner hadn't had the close relationship that only a husband and wife could have.

Had.

Michelle was gone. Jeremy was gone.

Emptiness consumed him.

His fingers crushed the empty can. Burying himself in the business wasn't working anymore. He'd been a fool to think it would work in the first place. Or maybe he'd been lucky it had lasted as long as it had.

Noah whistled for Houston so they could escape the four walls confining him. No matter what Brad said, he had no intention of flying Ruth or any other group of vultures around.

Chapter Four

Ruth watched the King Air touch down through bleary eyes as she stood by the window of the tiny shack located at an airstrip outside of Rio Salado City. At least the airplane brought a little lightness to the drab brown high desert surrounding the lone runway.

Fatigue wrapped around the muscle in her temple and yanked the pain winning out over the satisfaction of another successful coordination. Even her stomach was too tired to protest. How long would it take the pain relievers she'd taken with a sip of warm water to get rid of the migraine? Probably as soon as she got some sleep. And a decent meal. The sandwich from the hospital cafeteria left a lot to be desired, but at least her hunger had subsided.

Ruth disposed of the empty wrapper from the chocolate bar she'd bought for dessert from the vending machine into the garbage can as the aircraft approached. She didn't recognize the prop plane and wondered which company had come to pick her up—or more specifically, who piloted it.

"Bye, Joe. Thanks for waiting with me." She waved to

the staff employee from the hospital that had stayed with in her the tiny building that protected them from the elements.

She slipped out of the metal door, her footsteps echoing off the concrete still wet from the monsoon that blew through an hour before. Thankfully, she hadn't had to face the brunt of the storm outside while she waited for flights to resume so the pilot could land the plane.

After inhaling the fresh, damp smell, Ruth faltered about thirty yards from the aircraft. The staircase lowered from the plane, and a dog bounded down the steps.

"Houston." Pushing aside her exhaustion and headache, Ruth squatted down and held her arms open. The tiny dog jumped up, batted her with a muddy paw and licked her face. So much for her nice, clean shirt. "Oh, boy, I'm so happy to see you. How've you been?"

As she scratched the dog behind the ears, her heart skipped a beat. That meant Noah had come for her. She hadn't seen him since he'd changed her flat tire five days ago, and so much had happened in that time. Margaret Ann had taken a turn for the worse and succumbed to the infection Monday. Ruth was devastated at the loss. Then Tuesday the heart meant for Marissa had to go to another child because Marissa was too weak for an operation. Ruth wondered if the little girl would live to see her sixth birthday this weekend.

A tear crested her eyelash, but she shoved it away. God had a plan for everyone. Including Ruth. And Noah. At least Noah's familiar face was better than another anonymous one, even if only one of the plane's occupants was happy to see her. Scooping up the wiggly dog in one arm, she stood, hefted her duffel bag on her shoulder and stepped toward the plane and the man standing in the doorway who piloted it.

Sighing, Ruth grabbed the railing and pulled her body up the steps while her eyes skimmed over Noah's khaki pants, past his muscular chest underneath the green polo shirt he wore today and grazed his firm lips. Without his sunglasses on, Ruth noticed his blue irises deepened to the color of the clearing sky before they darkened like the receding monsoon clouds. The cold, remote look etched across his features signaled his attitude toward her profession hadn't changed much either.

Once Ruth stood next to him, Noah frowned and crossed his arms over his chest. He should have known Ruth would be the coordinator today. He didn't like the effect she had on him. She made him want to feel again. The call had come in right after Brad had lost the coin toss and had taken off on a scheduled trip to fly some executives to San Jose with the other pilot, Seth.

Hannah had left for another doctor's appointment, her second this month, which concerned him, but he didn't want to pry into his office manager's personal life, and Noah had been stupid enough to answer the phone instead of letting it go to the answering service. The only reason Noah was here was because he couldn't afford not to be. Turning down any job would put a strain on his business no matter what it cost his emotions. He'd deal with any repercussions after he paid his bills.

"Hi, Noah. Thanks for coming. I wasn't sure anyone would be able to get in with that storm."

"Ruth." His gaze raked over the blonde, taking in her appearance. Curly wisps of hair had escaped from her ponytail and framed her pink, heated face. Her white T-shirt covered now by his dog's paw prints made her look more like the girl next door that Brad had mentioned on their first fly-out together. Only the lab coat draped over her arm clued him in to her profession. "A little rain isn't going to keep me from my contractual obligations."

"Oh. Okay then. I'm glad of that. Well, thank you anyway." She glanced down and ran her fingers up and down the strap of her duffel bag.

Noah checked his resentment and wished he could retract those spiteful words. He hadn't meant to say them out loud. He hadn't meant to hurt Ruth. Using the tip of his finger, he tilted her chin back so he could lose himself in the color of her eyes that reminded him of the acres of green grass he'd mowed weekly on his granddad's farm. "I'm sorry, Ruth. That was uncalled for. Even if I didn't have a contract, I would have come for you."

Her expression softened to the caring one he associated with her. "It's okay, Noah. I know you have issues with my job. If you want—"

"No."

Ruth touched Noah's arm, the contact almost making him forget what she did for a living. "Whenever you're ready, I'll be here for you. Before I forget again, thanks for changing my tire Friday and for following me home."

"No problem. I'd do it for anyone." Noah shifted uncomfortably. He sure knew the right words to say today. Finding two coins in his pants pocket, he rubbed them together as silence loitered between the two.

"Where's the rest of the bunch?" Uneasy, Noah shifted his attention past her shoulder to the empty tarmac. He swatted at a lazy fly buzzing around his head. In the distance, monsoonal clouds were rebuilding behind the mountains.

"It's just me. I was on a case." Her voice hitched, signaling a death spiral to his resolve to remain unaffected by her charm. Would he ever be able to separate her from her job?

"A case?" A bead of sweat dripped into his eye before he could shove it away.

"I represented a local donor. Instead of bringing a team in to retrieve an organ, I came in by myself, found the recipients and coordinated the surgeries when the other teams arrived. What about you? Where's Brad?"

"I'm solo today, too. We're flying in a turbo prop that needs only one pilot. It saves money." Noah lost his battle not to get any more involved when he saw the fatigue clinging to the delicate skin under her eyes. He didn't recall seeing any flight requests by AeroFlight for Desert Wings Aviation in the past few days. "So how long have you been here then?"

"A little over twenty-four hours." Ruth's attempt at a smile failed to make it past her lips.

"Twenty-four hours? With no sleep?" Noah passed a hand across his face. Regardless what some people thought, he still had feelings. Lack of sleep made people careless and forgetful and maybe even a little overwhelmed. Especially doctors in residency at the hospitals in July. The worst time to be admitted. As if his wife and son had had a choice.

But then again, Ruth's patients were already dead. Or so the doctors claimed. Bile scraped the back of his throat.

The wail of an emergency vehicle careening along the empty stretch of highway to his left seemed to prove his point. His frustration mounted, but this time he kept his lips firmly shut. Desert Wings Aviation needed this contract.

"I'm used to long hours." Ruth's sigh drew an unwanted response from inside the wall surrounding his heart.

She was soft, sweet and vulnerable, in need of his protection. Wrong. So why the sudden need to wrap his arms around her waist and hold her close? Claim her warmth for himself and breathe in the clean scent he associated with Ruth. There was no way he would even contemplate falling in love again and risk losing her. Noah scanned the horizon. "We'd better get going before that storm decides to circle back for round two."

Once inside the plane, Ruth quickly buckled herself in the copilot's seat. Crazy to do so without Noah's permission? Yes. But she figured seeing what was in front of her might be easier than guessing.

Or maybe not. The tiny window didn't instill her with much confidence.

Neither did Noah's unyielding expression as he closed the door. So much for drawing some type of conversation out of him even if her tongue suddenly felt two sizes too big for her mouth. She knew it was crazy, but Noah's tenderness with her at the entrance to the plane affected her equilibrium.

Maybe she'd be better off in the back with Houston.

"Here. Wear this one." Noah crouched next to her, a headset in his hands. His expression softened as he gazed at her. She couldn't see his eyes because of the sunglasses he'd put back on, but she suspected they'd turned from ice to liquid pools of deep water.

His nearness affected her ability to take in oxygen. His fingers caressed a loose curl as he moved it out of the way. Then he placed the headset over her ears, his quickening breath like a gentle whisper. He stared at her as if memorizing every detail.

"Thanks." She tilted her head slightly and wondered briefly what it would be like to get a chance to know him outside of work. If she had the time. If she wanted to take another chance.

He wrenched his gaze from hers and moved away. He wasn't interested in her any more than she should be interested in him. If she'd learned anything from David, it was not to get involved with anyone who didn't share her beliefs, her values or her faith.

Ruth needed to focus on finishing her reports, not Noah.

Still, her gaze betrayed her. She watched, mesmerized as his long, lean fingers wrapped around his own headset and placed it over his ears. She remembered how he gently tousled Houston's fur and the careful way he treated his dog. She wanted that for herself.

"You decided to learn how to fly after all?" Noah's voice filled the sudden silence in her ears.

Ruth jumped and adjusted the volume.

"Wrong. I just thought since we were the only ones in the plane that it might be easier to sit up front."

Because against her better judgment, she needed to draw him out. She wanted to find some of the missing pieces of the Noah Barton puzzle that fascinated her. She pulled out her BlackBerry and a piece of gum from her purse.

"I could teach you."

But suddenly, Ruth wasn't sure what exactly Noah really wanted to teach her. The easy grin spreading across his face hit some turbulence. A jittery feeling erupted in her stomach that had nothing to do with the upcoming flight. Forcing oxygen into her lungs, she held it for a few seconds. As she released it, she pretended that all her fears rode the current of air she expelled from her body.

"Or maybe not."

At Noah's one-eighty attitude adjustment, she yanked off the wrapper and thrust the cinnamon flavored stick into her mouth. Then she started to search for an Internet connection on her BlackBerry to check her e-mails, even though she knew she was probably still in a dead zone.

"Please wait until we've landed before you turn it on."

"Right." Heat crept to her cheeks. Ruth knew the rules. She stared out the front window at the stretch of concrete as Noah set the plane in motion. Sitting up front gave her a much different perspective—to both pilot and the responsibility of flying a plane.

"Are you all set?" Noah's voice resounded in her ears again. The intimate tone surrounded her, the headset no barrier for her fragile heart.

"Ready when you are." Ruth squeezed her stress ball as Noah taxied onto the runway. The silent prayer she whispered every time she flew in an airplane crossed her lips. Bad idea to sit up front. The not-so-distant mountains loomed ahead like a plane-eating dinosaur. Whose brilliant idea was it to build an airport so close to a mountain range?

"Relax, Ruth. Everything will be okay. I'll keep you safe." Noah reached over and squeezed her fingers. "I promise."

Minutes later, Noah's hands strangled the yoke as the plane accelerated, the whiteness of his knuckles becoming a familiar sight with Ruth around. *I promise?* He wanted to cram those words back inside his mouth. He'd been saying the wrong things all day.

He hadn't kept Michelle and Jeremy safe.

He'd failed his own wife and son. He'd probably find some way to fail Ruth if he allowed himself to care for her.

In the corner of his vision, he saw her mouth chewing double time. He remembered her lips. Wide and generous. Made for kissing. He'd been a fool to touch her hand in comfort.

Concentrate. The plane wasn't going to fly itself.

At least he could control the plane and make sure he got Ruth back to the Scottsdale airport in one piece. The runway fell behind them, the surge he felt at every take-off crammed out all other emotions. A temporary calm seeped into his body with the increase in altitude.

"So, Noah, how did you learn to fly a plane?" Ruth's voice crackled in his headset, popping his peaceful vision.

"My dad taught me." He banked the plane north and slightly west. The woman had gotten inside his head while his guard was down. She didn't belong in there any more than she belonged inside his aircraft. He shouldn't have let her remain up front.

"Really? That's neat."

The softness in her tone threatened to draw him out. If he let her. He wouldn't. He couldn't.

He did.

"So your dad's a pilot, too?"

"Yes. But he's retired now." Thinking of his dad calmed him.

"That's cool how you followed in his footsteps."

"He thinks so, too." Noah's own questions gelled into his mind. He didn't want to know, didn't need to know, yet the sentences tricked their way into the stillness of the airplane. "What about you? Where you always a—" He paused a second, barely keeping the word *vulture* from passing his lips. "Coordinator?"

"I started as an O.R. nurse and then transferred to the ER. I came to the donor network just over two years ago."

"Interesting. What made you change?"

Ruth toyed with her bracelet. "The opportunity to do more for humanity."

Humanity. Right. As if that made her profession more

likable. More agreeable. More necessary. Ruth's moment of silence added another layer of emotion inside the aircraft. Another level of awareness to her vulnerability and his reaction to it.

"Do you always wear that bracelet? It doesn't distract you?"

"Yes and no, it doesn't. It was a present from a friend." Ruth didn't embellish her statement, but from the way her fingers touched one of the little multicolored butterflies, he suspected it wasn't an ordinary gift. Noah still carried a wallet-sized photo of the family portrait his wife had given him their last Father's Day together in a frame hidden in the pocket next to his seat.

"So did you always want to be a nurse?" Noah's question surprised him. He'd meant to remain silent for the rest of the trip, yet he couldn't stop the words from leaving his mouth.

"Did I always want to be a nurse?" Ruth repeated his question and appeared to think for a moment. A passion infused her and threatened to carry him along with it. "Yes. There's nothing more fulfilling or satisfying to know you've helped someone at the end of the day."

"I bet you were one of those kids who used to put bandages and slings on all your dolls."

He turned toward her just in time to see a blush creep into her cheeks. She twisted her lips before she bit down on the bottom one. "Well, my intentions were noble, but my actions weren't exactly."

"What's that supposed to mean?"

"I used my siblings a lot."

"That sounds dire." Noah eyed the instrument panel. The constant familiar of the screens and dials in front of him brought comfort. He'd loved sitting in the copilot's seat in his dad's plane learning everything there was to know about flying. About life. About love.

His parents' marriage still remained strong, while Noah's had barely lasted a decade. But the focus wasn't about Noah or his parents right now. It should be on Ruth and getting her back to Scottsdale as quickly as possible and out of his plane and out of his life. He didn't like the sudden camaraderie.

"It was dire. Just ask my brother, Robbie. I convinced him to put his finger in between the spokes of my bike tire before he spun it."

"You didn't."

"I did. He almost chopped it off." It wasn't satisfaction he heard in her voice but more disappointment and censure. Not something he associated with the woman sitting next to him.

"Remind me not to go bike riding with you." Noah's eyebrows raised a fraction. He wrapped his fingers around the yoke even tighter to keep from reaching for her hand. "How old were you?"

"Almost seven. Old enough to know better."

"You were still pretty young. How old was Robbie?"

"Four." Her sigh echoed inside the headset covering his ears. "But he'd just recovered from pneumonia. I was supposed to take care of him, not hurt him."

"I can't see you hurting anyone or anything. You were just a kid. I think you're being too hard on yourself." Against his better judgment, Noah reached over the console in between them and placed his hand over hers. His thumb traced the delicate skin on the back of her hand. Soft and smooth like Ruth. Her soft gasp filled his ears. He stopped short of lifting the tips of her fingers to his lips. "Did you get your brother's finger fixed up, or did he have to go to the hospital?"

"No, though it wasn't for lack of trying. I think I used every bandage in the house, too. My parents still had to take him to the emergency room with all us siblings in tow." At some memory, Ruth's lightly tinted lips created a welcoming smile. He liked seeing her that way. "Going anywhere with six children was always a trial."

"I'd say. I can't imagine going anywhere with a brood that size, much less a hospital." Noah gazed at her. "You loved fixing up your brother, didn't you? I can see it in your eyes."

"I did. I just wish I could fix everyone." Ruth paused.

Shifting uncomfortably, she pulled her hand from his, leaned behind her seat and then reached into her bag. The sudden loss of contact bothered him. A few misguided strands of hair tickled his arm before she tucked the strays behind the headset and he wondered how she'd look if she ever wore her hair loose instead of bound by elastic. He wondered how unbound curly, blond hair would feel in contrast to long, dark brown straight hair. He also wondered why he continued to think thoughts of Ruth outside the realms of work.

"Piece of candy? It's not chocolate, but it's still sweet."

After Ruth's fingers mangled the wrapper, Noah's voice dropped to a whisper, afraid she'd notice the tremor in his voice. "No thanks. So what happened to your brother's finger?"

"It's still a little crooked today, but he fully recovered and still blames me."

Noah stared out at the vast expanse of sky outside the tiny front window. This quiet, almost solemn woman made him even more uneasy. She affected him in more ways than he cared to admit and he wanted her smile to return. "At least you didn't draw a mustache on him in permanent marker."

"A mustache?" It worked. Ruth laughed at his outright suggestion. "Was it long and thin or big and bushy?" She glanced at him, and he knew she was trying to visualize the boy he'd been with marker in his face.

"She covered half my face. Right before all family photos, too. My mom still has that picture!"

She covered her mouth with her hand. "I'm sorry. I shouldn't be laughing, Still, I can't believe you'd allow that to happen."

Noah shrugged his shoulders. "What can I say? I was three and didn't know any better."

"So you have a sister who's quite a bit older than you?"

He noticed Ruth look around for a place to throw the empty wrapper. "Ten years. I was an oops baby. Here. I'll take that."

Noah held out his hand. After Ruth handed the crumpled cellophane paper to him, he tucked it in the small plastic bag hanging by his right knee.

"Thanks. Sometimes those are the best of all," Ruth said quietly. "All babies are a blessing no matter when they make their appearance."

Sweat gathered on his forehead. Needing to change the subject, he inhaled sharply and grabbed a lungful of Ruth. "So why are you so afraid of flying?"

Her laughter rang false. "What makes you think I'm afraid of flying around in a metal tube the size of a toilet paper roll that as far as I'm concerned defies the laws of gravity?"

Despite their recent exchange, Noah grinned at her choice of words.

"So have you always owned your own charter business?" Her question flipped the conversation back to him.

His gaze scanned the horizon again. "No. I flew for a commercial airline up until a few years ago."

Ruth's ability to draw the words out of him surprised Noah. His tongue responded to her question against his mind's better judgment, and he suddenly found the need to release things he'd kept locked for three years.

Communicating with Ruth wasn't as difficult as he'd imagined.

"What made you change?"

The words froze in his throat.

He left his employer right after the accident that changed how he viewed life and love and realized how short and meaningless his existence had become.

"It was time." Noah remembered kissing his young son goodbye. The inadequate feeling and guilt he felt watching a team of medical professionals assemble to take pieces of Jeremy and scatter them across the country bombarded him. He'd never learned what happened.

His stomach roiled at the thought of the letters forwarded afterward by the Arizona Organ Donor Network. He hadn't been able to read them. He couldn't throw them away, either, because he'd be throwing another part of Jeremy away, so he'd hidden them in a box in his garage. Noah pushed a tear away before it had the nerve to fall. When would the pain go away?

Chapter Five

Back on the ground, soft moonlight filtered in through the cockpit window, surreal and fighting for space with the overhead lights. Tiredness had crept in while Noah wasn't looking. His shoulder muscles felt like they were bunched into a pretzel.

No other planes fought for space on the runway, and he'd managed to land without incident despite the wet pavement. The water puddles around the Scottsdale airport glistened in the moonlight, and the fresh dampness seeped through the ventilation system. He loved the smell of the desert after a rain.

His gaze strayed to Ruth sleeping in the copilot's seat with his dog on her lap. Lucky dog. She'd fallen asleep halfway through the flight. Noah taxied to his hangar, parked and removed his headset. Wiping the sudden band of sweat from his brow, he looked over at Ruth's hands.

Short, manicured nails tipped her delicate, nurturing fingers. His hand inched toward hers in remembrance of how well her right one had fit inside his. He forced it to his side.

Noah unhooked his seat belt. Houston stirred and raced to the door, waiting for freedom. "Ruth. We're here."

Her figure remained motionless except for the rise and fall of her chest. The white shirt with Houston's muddy paw prints on the front accentuated the curves she usually hid. The sudden need for a glass of water consumed him. As if mere liquid could quench the thirst for human companionship Ruth created inside him.

"Ruth?" he said again, a little louder this time.

Still no movement from the other side of the plane but Houston whined at the confinement. "In a bit, boy. Just be patient."

Noah stretched and proceeded to scratch the needed data into his flight log. Anything to drag his attention away from Ruth. Too bad his eyes had other ideas.

He took another glance at his passenger, so still, so peaceful and definitely in need of sleep if she hadn't rested since she'd been dropped off yesterday. Much as he longed to deplane and call it a night, he didn't have the heart to wake her.

Noah settled back in his seat and looked at her. Houston stared back at him with a woeful expression underneath his shaggy hair. Noah's lips twisted into a wry smile. Pulling a dog treat from the box he kept by his seat, he held it out to Houston. "Come here, boy."

This time his dog obliged. "You're part cat, aren't you? Only willing to come if there's something in it for you."

Houston jumped up onto his lap, circled a few times and plopped down where he could still see Ruth. Noah scratched him behind the ears and sighed. "You like her, don't you?"

Houston whined, looking for another treat.

"Don't get any ideas." He whispered as his hand stilled on the warm, squiggly body.

He looked around the darkened plane, the one he'd christened *Michelle Marie.* His late wife's insurance payout had made it possible to start the business. He'd gladly give it all back to have his family by his side.

Nothing could ever make what he'd lost right. Nothing.

Especially the woman sleeping so peacefully in the seat beside him. Sometime during the flight, she taken out her ponytail and her riot of curly blond hair haloed her oval face. A dusting of freckles sprinkled her nose and cheeks. Not even remotely close to his wife's exotic dark looks and doe-eyed innocence. Where Michelle stood almost eye to eye with him, the top of Ruth's head barely reached his chin. He'd noticed that the first day he'd met her. His wife's slender, model-thin build contrasted with the nurse's soft, cushiony-in-all-the-right-places physique.

She interested him, but he couldn't do a thing about it.

He needed to get Ruth out of his plane—better yet, out of his life. Could his company survive if he cancelled the contract? Possibly, if he picked up two or three more. Would his friendship with Brad? Doubtful. They'd been through too much together, and he loved him like the brother he'd never had, but Brad would view canceling the contract as a betrayal.

Noah squeezed the bridge of his nose. The air inside the plane grew uncomfortable, and Noah needed to move before he nodded off like his passenger.

His nails dug into his palm. He concentrated on the pain and not the woman beside him. At the Rio Salado City airport, he'd noticed Ruth had dimples. Generous and deep, like the emotions he suspected she hid underneath her professional exterior. But it was an illusion.

Ruth was a person he couldn't understand. Another ambulance chaser, but she didn't want a lawsuit; she wanted body parts. Noah growled, causing Houston to jump from his lap.

Unable to remain seated, he unfolded himself from the seat, strode to the door and then lowered the staircase. Noah whistled to his dog. "Come on, boy."

Ten minutes later he stood over the copilot's seat. The longer he stared at the coordinator, the harder it became to remember Michelle. A connection lingered between them when he leaned over to gently shake Ruth's arm again. "Ruth? It's time to wake up."

Something warm settled on Ruth's arm. She lashed out at the object disturbing her sleep. Funny. She couldn't move.

"Ruth, wake up."

That most incessant voice peppered her dream of running through the fields near her parents' home near Milwaukee, Wisconsin, with Rachel. The Rachel that would always look eight years old, no matter how much Ruth aged.

"Go away. Leave me alone." She tried to turn over, but something constricted her movements. Panic set in and she started to thrash about.

"We're back in Scottsdale."

Ruth awoke with a start and stared into Noah's eyes. For a second, her lungs forgot to function as she allowed herself to be carried away by the current between the two of them. Her gaze slid to his rugged lips. The unspoken question of how they would feel against hers fizzled in the stillness of the night. Her cheeks burned with embarrassment. "Oh. Sorry. I must have fallen asleep. I'll be out of your way in a second."

But when Ruth's unsteady hands went to release the seat belt, Noah beat her to it. His thoughtfulness surprised her until his remote expression distanced her. After grabbing her duffel bag, she stood and then threw the strap over her shoulder. She moved to the door. "Thanks for the lift, Noah. I'll see you around."

As she clutched the handle on the staircase to keep from tumbling down the steps, a sense of déjà-vu engulfed her. With luck, only an impatient Houston greeted her and not another flat tire. At the bottom of the staircase, a huge yawn emerged. As long as things went right, she'd be home and asleep in thirty minutes tops.

"So did you get any rest in Rio Salado City?" Noah spoke softly from the top of the steps as if afraid to upset the stillness of the night.

Heat flared in her cheeks again. Her sleeping arrangements were not something she usually talked about with someone who wasn't a complete stranger, yet not a friend either. "I managed to rest a little at the hospital and while waiting for you."

Noah raked a hand through his hair and descended the stairs. "That's not enough. I'm almost finished here. Please let me drive you home."

Houston barked and jumped up on Ruth's leg, his tail wagging furiously behind him, his tongue dropping out of his smiling mouth.

"Look, Noah. I appreciate the offer, but that's not necessary. Unless I have another flat tire." Her sigh dissipated into the darkness. "I'm used to operating on little sleep. I'll drive myself home. Besides, I have somewhere important to be in Phoenix tomorrow afternoon, and I don't want to put you out or anything." She wouldn't miss her friend's funeral no matter how tired she was. Margaret Ann's loss had hit her hard. More sadness crept in and zapped any remaining energy. Her shoulders slumped.

"It is necessary. It's past midnight, and you look like you're ready to drop. I'll pick you up in the morning in plenty of time to get you where you need to be." After her nod, he pulled her duffel bag from her shoulder and slung it over his.

After securing the plane, he placed his hand on the small of her back and guided her to his truck, Houston running happily in front of them. Even in her fatigued state, she responded to his gentleness.

Silence surrounded them on the short ride. Even the dog remained quiet, occasionally popping his head up to look out the side window.

Outside her house, Noah parked his truck. He placed his hand on her arm to stop her from opening the door. His fingers touched hers for a moment, the contact comforting before his hand fell away to fish a flashlight from his glove compartment. "You should leave a light on."

Ruth groaned silently. As usual, she'd forgotten to leave the porch light on. She doubted nothing more than that crazed neighbor cat hid in the bushes, but it felt good to know Noah was with her and that despite his actions and expressions, he did care for her a little. "I appreciate your concern, but I don't like to waste electricity or broadcast that I'm not home."

"They make motion lights, you know." Noah got out of his truck and strode around to the passenger side to open her door. "Houston, let Ruth out."

After the dog jumped into the driver's seat, Noah helped her down and escorted her to the unlit front porch, his fingers cupping her elbow as if they belonged there.

"I'll keep that in mind. Usually it's not an issue." With the help of the beam from his flashlight, Ruth unlocked her door. Bleary eyed, sad and in need of human contact, she turned around and hugged him.

Noah almost imploded at her compassionate touch. Instinctively, he put his arms around her in return. He buried his nose in her hair, her unique scent mingling with the onset of early morning. He could get used to this. Forcing air from his lungs, he set her away.

"Thanks for the ride, Noah. It's been a rough day. I'm actually more tired than I realized. Bye."

Sadness hovered in the humid air around them. Her imperceptible nod told him she understood. When she stepped inside her doorway, loneliness scraped at his memories. He kidded himself into believing peace existed inside the four lonely white walls of his condo that mocked his attempt to lead a normal life.

"See you tomorrow. Call me when you're ready. I'll be at the office." Noah spoke to the white painted door, still feeling her warmth.

"Are you feeling okay?" Noah sat down on the edge of his office manager's wood desk. He carefully looked at Hannah. Dark circles under her eyes contrasted against her peaches and cream complexion, and she didn't have her normal sparkle.

"I'm just tired, that's all." Hannah's gaze fell over his right shoulder. Her hands trembled slightly as she toyed with the pen she'd used to make some notes on a recent contract.

Now that he thought about it, Hannah hadn't been herself for the last few days, but Noah had been focused on his own problems.

"Are you sure that's all?"

"Positive." She still refused to meet his gaze.

Noah knew the truth hovered behind her lips. But trying to get them to slip past the rigid wall the office manager erected would be harder than the home football team actually winning the championship any time soon.

"Maybe you should take a vacation day tomorrow."

"Oh, no. I'm fine. Really. I'll need my vacation time later in the year." A shadow of fear flickered across her features before she masked it with the cool efficiency that had won her the job as office manager.

Noah didn't deserve her.

Hardworking and honest to a fault, Hannah reminded him of someone else he knew, but that's where the resemblance ended. That's where he needed to end it.

The front door opened, and a deliveryman walked in. Houston barked. His short nails scraped against the Saltillo tile floor as he skittered into Hannah's lap.

"Some watchdog you turned out to be. Glad you decided to wake up," Hannah joked without her usual smile. Her hand rested on his dog's fur longer than normal as if his small, squirmy body held some sort of miracle cure for whatever ailed her.

Noah signed for the package. "Yeah, somehow he missed the attack first and ask questions later gene. I should have gotten a rottweiler."

"I'd like to see you get one of those up in your planes."

"That would be something, wouldn't it? Might scare the passengers though."

The driver dumped the box of office supplies on her desk and slipped out the door. As Hannah slit open the box with a pair of scissors, Noah continued to stare at her. She'd gained a little weight, or had suddenly decided to start wearing more loose fitting clothing. Was Hannah pregnant? That would make sense, but to his knowledge, the single mother never dated, choosing to spend her time with her ten-year-old son.

And it wasn't for Brad's lack of trying.

Noah glanced at his watch. "I think I'll keep Houston, though, right buddy?"

The phone on Hannah's desk rang. Noah noticed her fingers still trembled as she picked up the receiver.

"Desert Wings Aviation, Hannah speaking. How may I help you?" The office manager flipped to a fresh piece of paper on her notepad and grabbed a pen. Beneath her desk, Noah could hear Hannah's sandal click as she tapped her foot.

"Thanks, Ruth. I'll let Noah know. Goodbye."

Hannah's fingers remained on the phone seconds after she disconnected the call. Her face paled further as she briefly closed her eyes. "Ruth Fontaine is ready to be picked up?" Hannah opened her eyes and quirked her lips into a mischievous smile. "Since when did we start a shuttle service for the employees of our contracts?"

Noah squeezed the bridge of his nose, surprised that Hannah had relaxed enough around him after a year to tease him. He was going soft in his old age. "Since some of those employees have to work twenty-four-hour shifts and I figured it was safer to keep them off the roads. I think it also gives us an advantage over the other charter companies, too, don't you think?"

"Absolutely, Noah." Despite her obvious discomfort, Hannah's eyes danced in merriment.

He wondered how Ruth would look if she allowed herself to really laugh. So far he hadn't seen many reasons for that to happen, and suddenly, he wanted that to change.

"I'm on my way. It's almost lunchtime. Why don't you call it a day with pay and go spend some time with your son after school? Just forward the calls to my cell phone, and I'll grab them when they come in. I shouldn't be too long." Noah couldn't really afford to let Hannah go early but somehow in the past week a certain blonde had broken a tiny hole through three years of anger and bitterness, allowing him to start seeing the outside world again.

"Are you sure?" Relief flared on the delicate features of her face.

"Positive. You need it."

"Thanks." She blew out her cinnamon scented candle before she returned the pile of papers to her inbox and logged off her computer. When she leaned over to retrieve her purse, a tiny groan escaped her lips. Something was definitely wrong, but Hannah waved off his offer to help her up. "I'll see you tomorrow morning."

"Bye."

Noah stood by Hannah's desk, staring at the saguaro cactus outside the window minutes after her compact car left the parking lot. He'd done the right thing, yet the emptiness in the office bothered him. As he grabbed his hat, whistled for Houston and locked the front door, he sensed his carefully constructed world was crumbling around his shoulders and he didn't have enough emotional cement anymore to build it back up.

Somehow, Ruth Fontaine was involved whether he liked it or not.

A few moments after Ruth hung up with the woman who answered the phone at Desert Wings Aviation, she pulled the sleeveless black dress she'd worn too many times this year already over her head. Death was a part of life, and also part of God's plan, but it didn't make it any easier to say goodbye to another friend. Ruth, as well as the rest of the volunteers, staff and children would miss Margaret Ann terribly.

After twisting her hair into a knot, she clamped it down with a clip, sprayed on hairspray and patted down the curly wisps that refused to conform with the styling mousse. Not that it would really matter because by the time she got to the church the strays would have worked themselves free again.

She sighed and put on her jewelry, slipped on her sandals and added some tinted gloss to her pale lips. Then she headed to the kitchen where she stuffed the obituary and directions to the gathering afterward into her purse and made sure she had her car keys.

Ready, Ruth hovered near the front door. The neighbor's cat sat perched in the tree outside her office window, feeding her sadness. What poor, innocent animal was on its snack list today? She really wished Boots would take up residence somewhere else.

A flash of white caught her eye, and she sucked in her breath.

Her grandfather's old clock chimed noon. Noah's punctuality surprised her. She'd only called twenty minutes ago, figuring she'd have to wait at least an hour before he showed up. Ruth released the frilly white lace curtain over the side window, unlocked the door and stepped outside into the hot sunshine. Noah opened his door and let Houston jump down before he followed suit.

"Good afternoon, Ruth." His lips cracked from their straight line into a frown as he gazed down at her. "You look nice today. Special occasion?"

"Hi, Noah. Hi, Houston." Ruth scooped up the happy, squirmy dog but stopped him from licking her carefully made-up face. After she set him back on the walkway, her fingers brushed away a few strands of dog hair and smoothed out the nonexistent wrinkles on her black dress.

Ruth felt her sigh all the way to her toes. "You might

say that. As soon as I pick up my car, I'm going to a funeral."

A stagnant moment of silence hung between them.

Noah rubbed a bead of sweat from his forehead. "I'm sorry. Close friend?"

"Yes. I wouldn't be where I am today if it wasn't for Margaret Ann." Ruth bit her lip. She was not going to break down in tears and test her new waterproof mascara. She was going to keep her emotions bottled up like the man standing in front of her.

Yet the next thing she knew, Ruth was in his arms, clinging to the front of his polo shirt. His arms cradled her as they had last night and it felt so right; yet she could still sense him trying to withdraw. Her cheek caressed the soft tan material covering his muscled chest. She swore she heard his heart beat as she gasped for air. His masculine, just out of the shower scent, hovered around her. "I'm really sorry, Ruth."

Beside them, Houston barked, bringing the moment to an end. The warmth lingered where his arms had wrapped around her, but he maintained a silent, emotional mile away.

Ruth pulled away. "Thanks for coming to pick me up. My garage was feeling a little empty this morning."

In reality, her two-car garage was always half-empty. But Noah's truck wasn't the cure to filling it up. Ruth didn't need any more complications or problems than she already had. Her gaze skimmed the form-fitting polo shirt that accentuated his perfectly sculpted pecs. Her gaze focused on Houston instead of staring at Noah as if he were the proverbial last man on earth.

"Do you always bring your dog with you?"

"Most of the time. He gets lonely when I leave him behind. I hope you don't mind."

"Not at all. I love Houston." Though Ruth wondered if Houston was really the lonely one.

"Nice place. I didn't see much of it last night when I dropped you off." Noah surveyed the slump block home.

"Thanks." Ruth swelled with pride. She'd worked hard the past few days to maintain her home despite her crazy hours. "It suits me. The only thing it doesn't have is a pool. Too much work."

"You live alone?"

"Yes." For a second, Ruth wondered if he had an ulterior motive for asking that question. Probably not. She buried her disappointment. Still, her gaze slid past his ringless hand before she eyed the newly cut bougainvillea bush to her right. The scratches on her arm had healed, but the memory of fighting with the thorny branches almost made her eyes water.

"Ready to go? I wouldn't want you to be late."

"Of course." After locking the house, Ruth followed Houston inside the truck. She clicked the belt in place with a sudden sense of déjà-vu. "Thanks for picking me up. You really didn't have to. I could've found my own way."

Noah buckled himself in and flipped the key. "Not necessary. It's another perk we've decided to add to our services."

The all-business, no-nonsense Noah was back.

"Well, thank you anyway." The cold air-conditioning blasted against her heated skin, and she focused on the rest of her day. After she paid her respects to Margaret Ann, she'd stop by the Children's Center and surround herself in the Lord's work and bring happiness and peace to those who welcomed it. Noah needed it, too, but until he allowed Him into his life, Ruth could only pray for him to find his way. His salvation.

Her thoughts quieted when she realized she had bigger things to think about. Something wasn't quite right when they reached the airport parking lot. She blinked.

"Did you get a new car?" Noah gestured to the four vehicles scattered in the lot, almost as if parking next to each other was a sin.

A red Jaguar, a white Mercedes, a silver Volvo and another white pickup truck. Her stomach flopped worse than if they'd hit turbulence. "No."

Chapter Six

From the passenger seat of Noah's truck, Ruth pointed to a spot where she'd carefully parked her car. Or at least she thought she had. She rubbed her forehead in an insane attempt to recall where she'd left it, since she'd had a lot of things on her mind the other afternoon.

"Where's my car? The parking lot's not that big." Her stomach roiled. Where was a biohazard bag when she needed one? She'd rather face all the turbulence the weather could throw at her than the realization that someone had stolen her car. "I left my car over there. I know I did."

Noah maneuvered his truck around a dented light pole and pulled in the spot next to where she had pointed.

"Wait." Noah stopped her from opening her door. His fingers touched hers for a moment, the contact making her more aware of the single, table for one status of her life even though that's the way she wanted it. Her gaze skimmed his broad shoulders after he got out of his truck and strode around to the passenger side to open her door.

"Thanks." Ruth jumped down onto the hot pavement and scurried past him. "Of all the lowdown, rotten—"

She kicked the glittering shards of glass that marked the spot where she'd left her Accord Wednesday afternoon and disrupted a flock of pigeons. A hot gust of wind played with a discarded plastic cup near the fence. Ruth reached for her stress ball only to discover she wasn't wearing her lab coat. Of course not. It was her day off and she had other plans. Plans that included comforting those in need like Margaret Ann's family. Like her kids in the Children's Center.

Digging through her purse, she found a piece of gum. Chewing helped relieve her stress, too. She plopped the cinnamon flavored stick into her mouth and chewed double time to soften it up. Maybe this was just a reverse mirage. Maybe the shimmery image where the sun beat down on the cement had hidden her car behind a veil of something and in less than a minute, she'd be behind the wheel, blasting the air-conditioning and on her way.

She stared at the spot in front of her. Nothing. Her stomach sank to the tips of her black sandals. "I can't believe someone stole my car. Why would someone steal a regular car instead of the Jaguar?"

"It probably wasn't left overnight," Noah responded with a sigh.

"Oh. Good point."

From inside the truck, Ruth heard Houston give his comment in short, static barks. Turning away from Noah, she paced around the empty parking space marked by three white lines. In the bright sunlight, the glass shards winked at her, mocking her attempt to remain composed. How was she supposed to pay her respects to Margaret Ann when she had no way to get there?

"Think." Ruth continued her march around in a circle, tapping her fingers against her forehead. "There's got to be a way. An answer. A solution."

She stopped in front of Noah again and stared at the smattering of dark hair showing from the V-neck of his polo shirt. She swallowed. As her gaze locked on her reflection in his sunglasses, a stillness pushed her chaos away. *Okay, Lord. I get it. You do have a sense of humor today. Noah's hurting and you want me to help. Since when did you become a matchmaker though? And what if I don't want to play along?*

Noah squeezed the bridge of his nose and stared at the woman standing in front of him. At least she'd stopped tapping her forehead. The action reminded him of something his grandmother used to do when she was thinking.

"Why don't you call your insurance company? I'll call the police."

Ruth's lost expression made another brick fall from the wall around his heart. A band of sweat glistened on her brow. According to the digital thermometer on the billboard some fifty yards away, the temperatures had already surpassed the triple digit mark. Concern for her well-being overrode all every other emotion fighting to dominate his thoughts. "You might also want to get back into the truck to keep cool. This could be a while."

Noah watched Ruth's hips sway underneath her black dress as she walked to his truck. Then she hoisted herself onto his passenger seat, settled the tan bag on her lap and pulled out her wallet and phone.

With her elbows resting on her knees, Ruth held the phone to her ear. She scrunched her brows together and tapped her delicate fingers against her forehead as she waited.

Noah felt bad. He'd insisted she leave her car overnight, and it had been stolen. He turned his back before he let guilt consume the last few rational thoughts he had in his head. And before he had any ideas of getting involved with a woman who wasn't his type—could never be his type.

After reporting the stolen vehicle to the Scottsdale police, he snapped his phone shut and retreated to the sliver of shade given off by the light pole next to his truck. The idea of taking a dip in his condo complex pool later planted itself in his brain after the police took Ruth's information and after Noah got back from taking her to a funeral he didn't want to go to but had unwillingly committed himself to.

"Noah?" Ruth slid off the seat and approached his tiny section of shade. Her sigh danced up and down the back of his neck. "I'm sorry about earlier. I had no reason to snap at you. Or blame you. According to my insurance agent, there's been a rash of thefts lately. I need to call them back when I get a police report number."

Righting himself from where the metal had burned into his back, Noah faced her. "Your apology's not necessary. If I hadn't insisted on driving you home last night, your car would be parked in your garage."

"Would it?" She planted her hands on her hips.

"Of course." Noah pushed an errant strand of Ruth's hair behind her ear. It was as soft as it had been last night. He suppressed the itch to caress the tiny pulse in her throat with his lips. He needed to remain detached.

Mercifully unaware of his thoughts, Ruth charged on. "But did you see it Wednesday when you came back? Or yesterday when you flew out? There's no telling when someone took it."

Instead of focusing on her lips, he finally focused on her words. Ruth had a point.

"I don't know. I wasn't paying attention."

Her hesitation cost him another piece of sanity. It added another layer to that chivalrous side he couldn't ignore.

"Look, Noah. This wasn't part of the plan. You've probably got other things to do. I'll call a cab to take me to a rental car place when I'm done here." Ruth now stood behind the open door and swung her purse strap over her shoulder. "Then I'll find my way to the cemetery."

"I don't have anything to do today that can't wait. All the office calls are being forwarded to my cell phone, and Houston would have been disappointed in me if I left you out here by yourself to deal with this." Noah wanted to reach out and hold her hand in reassurance. Who was he kidding? He was the one who would be disappointed if he didn't stay to help.

She simply stared at him, her lightly glossed lips pressing into a straight line.

Noah wedged a hand in his hair. "Look. The police are going to be a while. I suggest we go wait inside one of the buildings where it's cool so my truck doesn't overheat. I'll take you to pay your respects to your friend once you've filed the report, and then we'll go rent you a car."

"This isn't your fault."

"I say it is. Come on, boy." Chivalry wasn't dead as long as Noah could still breathe. Especially where Ruth was concerned. She brought out emotions he'd thought buried with his wife. He leaned inside the truck to shut off the ignition. His hand shook when he turned and slid his palm under Ruth's elbow to escort her to an air-conditioned building. He inhaled her sweet scent but bit down on his tongue to keep from burying his nose in her hair. The heat had gotten to him.

She made him want to care again.

* * *

"Where's the funeral?" Cloying heat and diesel-laden air surrounded them as Noah helped both Ruth and Houston into the truck after the police had come and gone. While the officers had handled the theft in the airport parking lot with efficiency, Noah didn't have much confidence they'd find Ruth's car. Or if they did, how much of the car would be left. Guilt assuaged his conscience again.

After Ruth glanced at her watch, she buckled herself in. She sighed with sadness, and tears pricked the back of her eyelids when she briefly closed her eyes. "It's too late for that. The funeral procession is probably halfway to the cemetery by now. Look, please drop me off at the car rental place. I can take it from there, Noah. Houston looks like he's ready to go home."

"Which cemetery?" Bile hit the back of his throat. Sometimes he wished he didn't have such a sense of chivalry—or in this case, a misguided sense of duty.

Ruth studied him so intently that a blush found a home on his cheeks. "If you insist. Phoenix Memorial. Thank you. I can still pay my respects and say goodbye."

"You're welcome." Noah straightened and narrowly missed hitting his shoulder blades on the passenger door of the truck.

A commuter jet touched down, the noise creating static in his mind. Noah used the time to walk around his truck and jump in the driver's seat. He started his truck and flipped the air-conditioning on full blast to dispel the heat. Houston jumped from the backseat and planted himself on Ruth's lap and stared out the front window as if daring Noah to dislodge him.

"Do you know where the cemetery is?"

Noah nodded and pulled out onto the side street that wound through the airpark businesses before turning north on Scottsdale Road. He knew only too well where he was going. He visited there twice a week if not more, depending on his schedule.

Finally at their destination after a slight delay on the 101, Noah stopped his truck several yards from the large group of mourners assembled under a canopy, spilling out into the shade of an old eucalyptus tree. The green fabric offered only moderate protection for the people from the sun filtering in through the tree branches above. Sweat formed under his arms when the crowd shifted, and he caught sight of the casket and the clergyman standing at the head of it.

The elderly, white-haired man in black glanced over at the truck, his gaze catching Noah's and his wise, aged eyes and open arms inviting Noah to join them. Join Him. Come back to the flock. Noah's grip tightened on the steering wheel. No. He wouldn't go back. Couldn't. God had forsaken him. He'd left him to wander around without the people he loved, who ironically Noah had buried a few hundred yards down the road.

"Thanks for bringing me. I'm sure I can catch a ride from here." As if sensing Noah's distress, Ruth reached over and placed her hand on his arm. Warm and full of life and love. All of the things Noah was not these days.

"I'll be waiting in my truck over there." Noah managed to control his anger and bitterness as he pointed to a pull off not too far away. The woman beside him was not responsible for what had happened. Not really. That was between him and God. And the drunk. And the doctors. And the woman with the red lipstick. Yet Ruth was one of them and not one of them. Would he ever be able to separate the caring, compassionate woman from her profession?

"But—"

"You'd better get out. It looks like they're waiting for you."

Once the group welcomed Ruth into their midst and she disappeared from view, Noah put the truck in Drive and slipped away. He'd meant to head to the spot where he'd told Ruth to meet him, but his heart had other ideas and he found himself parking even farther down and walking toward Michelle's and Jeremy's graves.

Houston trotted ahead of him, yet he didn't bark, as if sensing the solemn occasion. The dog sniffed between the two markers and then rolled on the freshly mown grass covering Jeremy's grave. Houston remained the only bright spot in Noah's day. Denial singed the surface of his heart. Who was he kidding? Ruth brought a bit of light into his dark world, too.

In the background, he heard the constant hum of traffic from the freeway and the din of lawn mowers in another section of the cemetery. Birds chirped from the tree branches overhead, and an occasional rabbit munched on the green grass. A few other families tended similar sites but off in the distance. Good. Noah liked to keep his visits private.

"Hi, Michelle." Noah felt his voice break, as he knelt between his wife and son's markers and brushed away a few stray grass clippings the landscapers had missed from Michelle's. "My sister called the other day. Her daughter got her first job as a cashier at the local community college. You remember Stephanie, don't you?"

No answer, but Noah was used to the one-sided conversations. "Of course you do. Well, Nancy's really freaked out about Steph working with college boys, but our niece is sixteen. The work will be good for her. And

Nadine's husband, Tom, is going through some sort of mid-life crisis and just bought himself a red Corvette."

Noah leaned over and adjusted the fake flowers in the permanent receptacle so they stayed upright. Houston sniffed at them until a pigeon distracted him and he chased it into the tree branch overhead. "Did you notice I replaced the flowers last month? They're your favorite."

He touched one of the yellow petals of the tulip, the silk texture a little rough between his fingers. They didn't last very long in the valley heat. He sat back on his heels and rubbed his palms against his jeans and wondered what type of flower Ruth preferred.

He clamped his teeth together. He didn't want to know. Michelle had been the love of his life. Only she mattered. But he had a hard time remembering what his wife looked like. The picture of the woman in his mind stood at another funeral only a few hundred yards away. He savagely plucked a few more stalks of uncut grass the mowers had missed and threw them to the side.

Despite the heat, the action felt good. It burned at the restless energy built up inside him. He would not think of Ruth. Or her laughter or the dimples that graced her cheeks when she gave him one of her smiles. He would not allow himself the opportunity to care for her. Because that could only lead to disaster. And heartache. And potentially another tragedy.

Twisting to his right, he attended to Jeremy's marker, shoving all thoughts of Ruth from his mind. She didn't belong there. Not now, not ever. He flicked off an errant clump of dirt from the J in Jeremy's name. "Hey, sport. Your favorite ball team is playing really well this year. There's some talk they may actually make the play-offs."

Moisture gathered in Noah's eyes. "They might even make it to the World Series again."

What happened to his family wasn't fair. He should be out playing ball with his son, not visiting his grave. He should be making plans to attend a baseball game instead of wiping the tears from his cheeks. He should…should have. Would have. Could have. A sigh rattled his bones. None of this was going to change anything.

Noah needed to let go. Move on.

If he could.

"Goodbye, Ruth. Thanks for coming." Margaret Ann's daughter, Fiona, wiped her tear-laden eyes as they stood under the canopy tent erected by the cemetery staff to shade them. "I really appreciate it. I know my mom does, too."

With less than a handful of mourners remaining, Ruth stopped, enveloped the slight woman in her arms and hugged her gently. Disappointment still lingered, but Ruth knew Margaret Ann's memory would live in her heart forever. "I'm sorry I was late and missed the beautiful service. Take comfort in knowing she's at peace now."

"And she's up in heaven with all those children she adored."

Ruth squeezed Fiona's hand. "Please let me know if I can do anything for you. Anything at all."

"I will. Thanks."

Fiona's husband of twenty-five years wrapped a comforting arm around his wife. "Are you sure you won't join us back at the house for refreshments? You're more than welcome to bring your friend along."

"Friend? He's more of an acquaintance, though sometimes…" Ruth's gaze swept across the cemetery grounds dotted with shade trees and a few benches until she spied Noah off in the distance with Houston at his side. Even from this distance she could sense his pain with his slumped shoulders and bowed head. Her heart ached for him. She'd started to care for the pilot and wanted to help him through whatever nightmares tormented him. "Really. I'd love to, but I can't. Unfortunately, I've got some unexpected business to take care of. Thanks though."

Ruth walked away from the grave and stayed on the grass until she'd passed the last parked car along one of the single lanes of pavement that wound through the cemetery. Finally, she cut across the road. Her heels clicked against the asphalt, creating a static rhythm until she reached the other side. She passed a few cemetery maintenance workers taking care of what looked like an irrigation issue. What had Noah so upset?

Only one way to find out. Ruth walked quietly to where Noah now knelt, his fingers tracing the inscription on a grave marker. As she read it, heaviness descended on Ruth, pushing away any chance of feigning ignorance. She swallowed her sob. At least she had her answer to his ever-present sadness.

Ruth's vision clouded. Michelle Barton. Loving wife and mother. She'd died a little over three years ago just shy of her thirtieth birthday. Her gaze skittered to the next marker. Seven-year-old Jeremy Barton died two days after his mother.

She wiped the tears away with her finger.

A hot, dusty breeze kicked up and played with Houston's curly hair as he sat next to his owner. Ruth reached out to touch Noah's shoulder. Would Noah welcome her comforting gesture? His muscles bunched beneath her palm and yet his hand reached up and covered hers for several heartbeats as if afraid to let go.

"Please. Don't. I can't." Noah finally pulled away and shoved a stiff hand through his hair. The blood leached from his face and a nerve ticked along his jaw.

Ruth gasped and dug her short, manicured fingernails into her palm. She'd overstepped her bounds. "I'm sorry for your loss, Noah."

Noah's stony silence unnerved her. Seconds ticked by. Then a minute. Only their ragged breathing and the sound of a passing car leaving the cemetery filled the air between them.

His sadness and hurt clung to her. Ruth stumbled away from the bleakness etched in Noah's features when he twisted around to look at her. He created a symphony of emotions inside her heart with disastrous results.

He stilled loved his wife.

"Ruth. Wait." Struggling to his feet, Noah whistled for Houston. The terrier dashed after Ruth and beat her to the white truck parked in the shade cast by a row of tall, thin trees. His short, yappy barks seemed to be trying to convey all of Noah's thoughts, but the dog apparently did a much better job. Ruth scooped him up in her arms and cradled him like a baby.

When the dog licked her face, Ruth's cautious laughter filled his ears and her hesitant smile chipped at the darkness embedded in his brain. Noah's footsteps slowed with each step. The hot afternoon sun beat down on his head and shoulders, making him even more uncomfortable as he clicked his remote and unlocked the doors.

Finally at her side, he stopped Ruth from touching the passenger side handle. "Look. Ruth, I—I…please look at me."

Ruth complied and tilted her head back to gaze up at him. Nothing but her soft, feminine features filled his vision. A tiny pulse beat wildly in her neck, and her wide generous lips lifted at the corners. Her unique scent blended with the freshly mown grass, wreaking havoc with his equilibrium. Noah found himself slanting toward her. It wouldn't take much to forget why he shouldn't get involved.

Noah swallowed and spoke before he lost all reasoning. "For some crazy reason I'm drawn to you, but I'm not looking for a relationship right now. I'm not ready."

"I'm not looking either." Ruth's whisper held a trace of regret. "Let's see if we can be friends then."

"I'd like that." Noah leaned around her, opened the door and helped her inside. His lips came within centimeters of grazing the top of her head. Who was he kidding?

Chapter Seven

The tension that started at the cemetery continued to rest on Noah's shoulders five minutes later as he merged back onto the freeway. Friends? Had they just agreed to be friends?

Friends should be able to talk about anything. Anything at all. So why did he struggle to ask the question that had plagued him for three long years. A question he wasn't sure he wanted answered yet still he had to know.

His attention flipped between his rearview mirror and the side one. Flashing lights of an emergency vehicle caught his eye. His stomach clenched as he flipped on his blinker, slowed down and moved over to the side. An over-size SUV with the AeroFlight name and logo careened by, adding to the tension inside the cab.

"Looks like someone from your office is working today." Noah's sarcasm slipped out before he could clamp his lips shut. His grip tightened on the steering wheel. Ruth deserved time off. She'd just worked over a twenty-four-hour shift. She'd just said goodbye to a friend. She'd just made a liar out of him because he was more interested in her in a not-so-friendly way. "Sorry. That was uncalled for. Anyone you know?"

"They went by so fast I couldn't tell, but it was probably Natalie Stanton. I think she was the on-call person today." Ruth leaned forward and adjusted the air-conditioning vent away from her.

Noah turned the air down. "The tall brunette?"

"Yes."

He heard Ruth's disappointment in that one syllable word. His mood grew even darker. On the last fly-out, Natalie had taken a sudden disliking to him because he didn't respond to her flirting. And it wasn't just because of what she did for a living. He'd tried to let her down gently, but he sensed he hadn't heard the last of her. "Don't worry. She's not my type. She asked me out, and I turned her down."

Seeing the Scottsdale exit ahead, Noah put on his blinker, checked his rearview mirror and slid back into the right lane. He didn't have much time. Despite the cool air inside the truck, a bead of sweat trickled down his forehead. It was now or never. "What does death feel like?"

"Death?" Ruth's hand stilled on Houston's back, and her fingers entwined in his fur. *Death?* Her heart took up residence in her stomach. This was not a conversation she'd ever expected to have with Noah. She adjusted her seat belt as if to anchor her more firmly into her seat.

"I don't know, Noah. I've never died before."

"But you've had experience with it." As they waited for the light to turn green at the bottom of the ramp, Noah's lips thinned as he looked at her, his skin taut over the hard planes of his cheeks.

She couldn't see the bleakness in his eyes because of the dark sunglasses, but she knew it resided in the deep, blue orbs. Ruth digested his words carefully. This had to have something to do with Noah's wife and son. The need to put his mind at ease consumed her.

"I know about physical death, Noah." She touched his forearm, and like clockwork, the muscles bunched beneath her hand. "All biological functions cease. I don't know how it feels though, but I suspect each one of us will approach death differently. For some it will be quick. For others, it could drag on for months or years."

She shuddered and squeezed her eyes shut. Rachel's smiling face stared back at her. A healthy-looking Rachel, not the thin, sick child she'd been before death finally released her spirit into God's hands. Her twin had suffered so much pain in the end; her passing had been a relief. Bonnie's death, too.

"Death can also be a blessing. It's part of the process of life. Every one of us will die." Ruth opened her eyes and stared at Noah, but his attention was back on the road. Traffic on Scottsdale Road was always a nightmare at this time of day, and she stared out at a sea of brake lights. "Sometimes it happens earlier than planned so it's important how you choose to live the life given to you."

Noah didn't comment on her dialogue, yet his remote expression had returned and his skin paled in the mid-afternoon sunlight. "That's not what I really want to know. Maybe I should have been more specific. What happens to a donor when they die? What does death feel like for them?"

Ruth chose her words with caution as alarm bells rang inside her brain. His question made her suddenly suspect that either his wife or son or both had been organ donors. Otherwise, why else would Noah ask?

"When a donor dies, he or she experiences what's

called brain death. It's the irreversible end of a person's brain activity."

"Is there much pain?" Noah's voice cracked.

Ruth stared at the anguish and pain etched into his features as he struggled with the conversation. She longed to free him from his demons.

"Noah, donation coordinators are called in after the donor is declared brain-dead by a physician. By the time we arrive, there is no pain, no reflexes, nothing. What is this all about?"

"Nothing," Noah whispered harshly.

Ruth knew she had to give him more time. She bowed her head, clasped her hands and said a silent prayer.

"How can you believe in God when you act at playing God with what you do?" Noah pulled into the rental car lot and parked in a shaded spot not too far from the entrance.

"Playing God? Is that what you think I'm doing?" Ruth's blood ran cold as she unbuckled her seat belt. He still couldn't accept her job despite what she'd told him. "I don't believe I'm playing God at all. I'm an agent of life. We live in a broken world, Noah, in case you hadn't noticed. I'm simply giving someone a second chance when the person who has died is already gone."

"Then how do you explain how donors are chosen?" His tone raised gooseflesh across her bare arms.

"How donors are chosen? You honestly think—" Turning to face him, she clenched her fists. A tear slipped down her cheek. Even after the few recoveries Noah had flown and the staff he'd met, he still didn't get it. She suspected he didn't want to get it. "You really don't understand the process at all."

She sensed a war raging inside him when Noah glanced

over at her. "No, I don't. All I see is a group of medical staff hovering around like vultures watching and waiting to divvy up parts to the highest bidder."

Vulture. Ruth stared at the man. Sorrow touched her. She couldn't reconcile this hard, bitter man with the one who'd so tenderly cradled her in comfort earlier.

"No one is chosen for death before they actually die, Noah. It's unethical. It's not like, oh, here's a healthy twenty-two-year-old. Gee, he'd be a great match for a couple of kidneys and a heart that guy needs in room 4. Let's not try our hardest to save his life so we can harvest his organs. It *doesn't* work that way."

Her fingers tightened around her purse strap, rivaling the color of the tan leather. Ruth bit her lip. Noah's reaction confirmed her earlier suspicions that someone close to him had been a donor. "I can understand your reaction, Noah, and I'm sorry. I think a lot of people have that misconception. I don't want to hurt you, only help you. Can't you see that?"

"You have no idea what I went through."

Ruth reached out to touch Noah's arm again. "No, I don't know what you went through. But I know all about losing a close family member." Images of Rachel flitted through her mind's eye again, like a kaleidoscope of colors and shapes. Rachel laughing. Rachel running. Rachel and Ruth curled up in bed as they read a book together. "My twin sister died a long time ago awaiting a transplant before they became really routine."

Silence.

Ruth could almost feel Noah's guilt and his hostility. "Why did you sign the contract with AeroFlight then if you felt this way?"

"I didn't. Brad did. The only reason I'm doing it is

because I can't afford not to, not because of some misguided sense that it *benefits humanity*." Noah lashed out
at her, his words stinging like lemon juice on an open cut.

Ruth flinched. Noah hadn't come to terms with his loss.
Sorrow slipped down her cheeks. "One of these days I
hope you'll understand."

She would never give up helping people in need,
whether it was a recipient, a neighbor, a coworker or
leading someone to God. But until Noah opened his eyes
and his heart and accepted what she had to offer, there
could be no future for them no matter how she suddenly
wished there was.

An idea blossomed in her brain before she'd managed
to get out of his truck. Maybe if Noah understood more
about the process, things would somehow change between
them. "Noah, would you like to see exactly what it is that
I do for the Arizona Organ Donor Network sometime?

"Not interested."

Ruth turned to face him, compassion lacing her steady
voice. "I think you are interested, but you're too afraid to
know that what I do is create hope."

His features twisted in pain. "You may think you know,
but really you know nothing about me and my circumstances."

"I know that you're still grieving and in pain and only
want to help you. Please. As a friend. God wants to help
you, too." She wanted to help him understand and accept
God's love into his life so that He could carry Noah's
burden for him. But unless Noah made the choice himself,
there was nothing Ruth could do.

"God turned his back on me when I needed Him most.
I'm not going back."

Her voice softened as she kept herself from touching

him again. Instead, Ruth dug inside her purse and pulled out a tiny pamphlet distributed by her company.

"Here's some information that will explain the process."

"Why are you showing me this? I don't care. I don't want to see it." Noah grabbed the copy and crushed it without even looking at the words.

"I'm sorry my presence is causing you so much pain. I can handle it from here. I'll see you around."

Noah reached out, but Ruth had already opened the door and slipped away. He wanted to run after her and apologize, but his feet and tongue wouldn't cooperate.

He couldn't do it. He couldn't follow her inside the gray stucco building and betray his memories of Michelle. Ruth was and always would be an organ donation coordinator just like the woman to whom he'd signed over Jeremy's organs. He was a fool to think of her as anything else. He couldn't cancel the contract because Brad, Seth and Hannah depended on him to keep the company operating. But he also couldn't let Ruth go. It was as if his body had recognized what his mind couldn't.

He'd work through his issues. But what would Ruth think if she ever found out about the truth he'd buried so deep inside that not even his partner knew about? He still blamed the doctors for not doing enough to save Jeremy. But ultimately, Noah had signed his son's death warrant. And that guilt ate at his soul.

The trill ring of the phone forced Noah's attention back to work Friday. He stopped pacing the tile. It wasn't helping release his pent-up energy anyway. His gaze skimmed the perimeter of the lobby, which doubled as

Hannah's office, taking in the stack of payables that still needed to be filed. Not to mention the stack of unopened mail on his office manager's desk. He pursed his lips. It was unusual for Hannah to leave work piled up.

The phone rang again. Maybe it was a last-minute request by an executive needing to fly out for a weekend getaway. Both Brad and Seth were available and only a call away. Anticipation surged through his veins at the thought of a pending flight. Before the phone could ring again, Noah picked up the phone normally answered by Hannah. "Desert Wings Aviation."

"May I speak to Hannah Stevenson please?" A female voice inquired.

Disappointment at what he suspected now was a sales call lodged in his throat. His fingers strangled the black receiver. "She's at lunch. Is there something I can help you with?"

A terse silence hung in the air. The sound of shuffling papers and muted voices in the background caught his attention. His grip tightened as if trying to reach through the line to draw out the person on the other end. Noah stared at the half-dead ivy pushed behind Hannah's almost-empty tissue box. Something was going on with his office manager.

"No. I'll try her at home. But please let her know that Dr. Lewis's office called. It's important she contact us immediately. Thanks."

The click resounded in his ear.

A doctor's office?

Noah yanked out Hannah's faux leather chair and sat down. Not a pen or paper in sight. His stomach churning, he pulled open the drawer and rummaged for something to write the message on. Noah owned the office, but he still felt like he was invading Hannah's territory as he peered through her things. Instead of finding a blank pad inside, his fingers pulled out a thick stack of papers. Some sort of medical research papers by the look of it. His gaze skimmed the top article.

Polycystic kidney disease? He read on about the growth of cysts in the kidneys and how they affected kidney functions and end-stage renal disease. At the realization that Hannah's health issues had nothing to do with a pregnancy as he'd first thought, he frowned.

Shadows shifted across the wood desk as a cloud passed in front of the sun. Houston sneezed, rose from his spot by the office door and then padded across the floor to sit at Noah's feet.

Absently, Noah scratched his dog behind the ears as he continued to read. "Houston, we have a problem."

He grimaced at how that phrase coined all those years ago slipped so easily from his lips. Forcing his gaze away from the papers in front of him, Noah slid the chair back, disgust and concern fighting for space inside his brain.

"Hannah's sick." His voice crowded out the silence. Houston cocked his head and raised his ears as if listening. "And she doesn't have a lot of options."

Everything all boiled down to one of them.

A transplant.

Nothing short of receiving a donor kidney could cure the disease raging inside her body. A lump formed in the back of his throat at the twist of fate. He forced his clenched fists to relax as he stood. He paced from Hannah's desk to the window where he could see monsoonal clouds building to the east.

"Why didn't Hannah tell us about her health problems?" Great. He was talking to his dog again.

The sound of the front door opening interrupted the

silence and the turmoil of his thoughts. Houston ran to greet a tired-looking Hannah after she walked through and dumped her purse beneath her desk.

"Hannah, do you have a moment?" Noah motioned for her to follow him into the office he shared with Brad.

"Is there something wrong?" The office manager's face paled further, but she trudged behind him. Noah wondered how she managed to hold herself together as he sat down. One glance at her trembling hands pulling at a loose thread on her sweater told him she just barely did.

"No. Not really. Please have a seat."

Jittery, like one of his new student pilots, Hannah took a seat in one of the leather chairs across from him. His fingers drummed the oak surface of his cluttered desk. With no easy way to approach the subject, he decided to be blunt. "How long have you been sick?"

Hannah hung her head as her fingers mangled the tissue she held. "How do you know?"

"Your doctor's office called during lunch. I found the paperwork as I was rummaging around for paper to write you a note." Noah rubbed his forehead and leaned forward. The chair squeaked in disapproval.

She lifted her chin and leveled her gaze on him. "It's true. So what happens now? Are you going to fire me?"

A stunned Noah stared into the depths of Hannah's green eyes. Did he really present that image to the world? Did Hannah honestly think this would make a difference in their working relationship?

"No, Hannah. I'm not going to fire you. You're too valuable. I just want to know what's going on. How can Brad, Seth and I help you through this?"

Tears crested her lower lashes, and she reached over to pull another tissue from the box on his desk. "I'm not sure you can unless you've got a spare kidney lying around. I've got polycystic kidney disease."

Noah nodded for her to continue.

"It's genetic. I've known about it since I was old enough to understand. It's only gotten worse these past few years."

"For a while I thought you were pregnant."

A tiny smile curved her lips. "That would be simpler, wouldn't it? No, the cysts are huge. The doctor thinks my kidneys weigh about ten pounds each."

Noah didn't like the sound of that. "So you're close to the end stage. Does your son have it, too?"

"Yes, and no. Dylan tested negative. The doctor's office called to set up my surgery. They want to take my kidneys out next week." A fresh batch of tears spilled. "I have two options. Dialysis or transplantation. But I don't want to be tied to a machine for the rest of my life. I've been on the waiting list for two years though, and nothing's come available. The doctors can't wait any longer. Phoenix is a terrible place to be on a waiting list. I've been told my options are better in Florida because there are more donors there, but I won't uproot my son. He's been through too much as it is."

"I'm sorry." Stepping around his desk in a daze, Noah moved next to Hannah and awkwardly patted her back. He never knew what to say at times like this and sorry seemed pretty lame. He'd heard it too often after Michelle and Jeremy died to put much stock in it. "If you need me to do anything for you, just ask."

His mind had a hard time trying to wrap around the concept of what Hannah needed. He'd only seen one side of the process. But now, by some ugly twist of karma, he was about to find out about the other.

"Really?" Hannah grasped his hand. Her pale skin

blended in with the white of the walls behind her. "I do need you to do something for me then."

"What is it?"

"Pray for me? And if anything happens to me, I want you and Brad to take care of Dylan."

Pain radiated from Noah's heart. Hannah had no idea what she was asking. Not that it was her fault. His office manager didn't know about Jeremy or that he hadn't prayed since his death. Noah squeezed her hand back. "Where is he going to stay while you're in the hospital?"

"With a friend. Their number is on the sticky note on my computer. But that's only a temporary solution."

"What about his father?" Stupid question. If the man who fathered Dylan had any sense, he'd be an important part of the young boy's life.

Hannah hiccoughed. "He doesn't want anything to do with his son."

Noah closed his eyes briefly. If something happened to Hannah and she had no one to look after Dylan, the boy would either go to his father if they could find him or into foster care. Neither option was very appealing for the small, sensitive boy Noah had met those few times. He wouldn't wish that scenario on anyone.

He squeezed her hand again as if he could force the illness from her body.

"Look, Hannah. I'm sure nothing is going to happen to you. But if it makes you feel better, I'd be happy to take care of him. I'm sure Brad would, too. Now go home and start your weekend early. Rest and psych yourself up for surgery."

"Thank you. I don't know where else to turn." Another tear slid down Hannah's cheek after she squeezed her eyes shut. "I'm so scared."

I'm scared, too. But Noah knew better than to vocalize his thoughts. He'd read the stack of information Hannah had hidden in her desk. He knew without a transplant that her only other option was dialysis for the rest of her life, and she'd just said she didn't want that. So that left one option.

A transplant.

From a donor.

How could the God he'd forsaken be so cruel to take another young life? A single mother with a child?

Thankfully, Hannah had returned to her desk before she saw the confusion he knew had to be in his eyes. Long after her departure, he paced the tiled floor, stopping occasionally to stare at the picture of his plane on the wall. The sun shifted, its rays streaming in through the slated blinds, catching the dust particles in a macabre dance on their way to the floor. At the side of Noah's desk, Houston snored as his foot twitched.

A transplant. Noah should go to Ruth. He knew she'd help him understand the process. She'd already offered. His neck muscles bunched, and he pounded his fists against the wall waking his dog. A guttural cry burst through his lips. He couldn't do it. He couldn't wrap his mind around the idea that Hannah needed someone to die so she could live.

Someone like that boy on that first flight with Ruth.

Or Jeremy.

He turned around and slid down the wall. An agitated Houston licked his hand. He couldn't deal with this right now. Tomorrow. Or the next day. Or the day after that.

Chapter Eight

~

"Come on, boy. Let's get out of here and go to the park. I'll even let you chase a duck or two." Noah climbed into the driver's seat late Saturday morning and started the truck. He couldn't stay confined inside the walls of his condo anymore. Everywhere he turned, memories of Jeremy hovered. So did the image of Ruth trying to reach out to him.

A tiredness crept over him, courtesy of the sleepless night, but Noah knew it was from more than that as he pulled out of the condo complex. It was the three years of numbness, anger and guilt that wore his emotions thin.

At the park in central Scottsdale, Noah leashed Houston and pulled out a well-used tennis ball from underneath the passenger seat. Then he jumped down after his dog, the warm pavement hard underneath his feet. Inhaling the scent of the city and the aroma of grilling meat, they made their way to the grass lawn. Towering palm trees lined the parking lot while Palo Verde and eucalyptus trees created shade over picnic tables and benches.

Kids screamed and ran around and over the huge jungle

gym play area and swings as he walked past. Mothers, both with and without strollers, stood guard over their children as they talked about whatever women talked about these days. Michelle used to bring Jeremy to a smaller park closer to their home. Sometimes Noah would join them. Most of the time not. He'd been gone a lot during his son's youth and spent the rest of his time fixing up their old home. Sorrow gripped him again.

Noah finally settled himself under an old ironwood tree as far away from the play area and the section blocked off for the half dozen or so kids' soccer games. He unleashed Houston in the designated dog area. To his right, just past the slight crest of a small hill, a swollen man-made lake glistened in the sun while ducks preened themselves on the grassy shores or paddled around in the water.

He threw the small ball to Houston in the opposite direction to keep the dog's attention from the wildlife. Noah really didn't have any intention of letting Houston chase the ducks, regardless of what he'd said earlier. The poor ducks had enough trouble with the little kids teasing them with breadcrumbs and chasing them around.

Houston ran back to him, his tail wagging, his entire body shaking in anticipation as he dropped the soggy ball at Noah's feet. With a grimace, Noah picked it up again and threw it a little farther this time, his dog bounding after it at top speed.

A family with a toddler and a baby in a stroller passed by, the little boy squealing in delight at Houston's antics of playing keep-away with the ball. "You're enjoying this, aren't you?"

Houston barked. The dog nudged the ball toward him, but when Noah bent to retrieve it, Houston grabbed it with his mouth.

The boy approached, holding out his pudgy hands. Noah judged him to be about the same age as Jeremy was when they welcomed Houston into the family. Despite the warm sunshine and beautiful fall day, everything seemed to be reminding him of his son these days. Since Ruth, that job of hers and the contract came into his life. Somehow, the pain right now didn't seem as bad as it had been this morning. Or maybe he was just kidding himself.

"Looks like we've got a visitor, Houston." Noah motioned the boy over, nodding to his parents that it was okay. "He's friendly. Come say 'hi.'"

"Ball." The boy made a beeline for the wet tennis ball. After picking it up, he looked up at Noah with wide brown eyes. "Ball?"

Houston barked again and sniffed at the boy's hand, his wagging tail creating a breeze over Noah's bare arm.

"Sure you can throw him the ball." Noah smiled.

With Houston occupied, he sat back and tried to relax against the smooth bark of the tree. His mind refused to unwind. Ruth's anguished face hovered behind his eyelids, unwelcome and welcome at the same time. He hadn't really meant to hurt her with his words the other day. He had no excuse to allow the three years of bitterness and disappointment to overrule his professionalism. Everyone had a job to do. Even the tax auditor.

A cold nose nudged him underneath his hand and the wet ball dropped onto his lap. Noah noticed the little boy and his family's attention had moved to the ducks at the lake. But that wasn't what held his interest by the edge of the water.

"Look who's feeding the ducks, Houston. Hannah and Dylan." His office manager and her son sat on a colorful blue, white and green Mexican blanket by the bank, throwing breadcrumbs into the water. Houston whimpered and wriggled his tiny body in anticipation of another throw.

Noah obliged. Seeing Hannah and her son here threw him off guard. He knew he should walk over and say "hi," but he didn't want to intrude on their time together. The way they sat and talked reminded him that he and Jeremy used to do the same thing when Noah was home. Sometimes Michelle would join them, and the three of them would have a picnic on the postage-stamp grass area of their backyard, or climb a tree or play a quick game of croquet.

The special times. Things to be savored. Enjoyed. Like Hannah was doing. Creating memories for Dylan to carry with him his entire life, no matter what the outcome of Hannah's surgery next week.

Fisting his hands, Noah bit down on his lip to keep his emotions in check. Hannah would be okay. She had to be. She needed to live. She needed a second chance.

Jeremy hadn't been given one, but according to those unopened letters Noah received from the donor network, the four people who received Jeremy's organs had. By signing those papers, he'd created the miracle other families needed. If Ruth told him the truth, the doctors had done all they could to save his son.

A cleansing tear dropped onto his hand. Jeremy's life had even more meaning in death. And as long as Noah remembered Jeremy's organs helped others to live, his son still lived.

Noah bowed his head. He hadn't done this in years. He felt the need to do so now, but words wouldn't come. He didn't know what to say, how to reach out. He wasn't ready to talk to God again. He wasn't quite ready to forgive yet. But he was ready to start trying.

* * *

Present and car keys in hand Saturday afternoon, Ruth bumped into something solid and masculine on her way out her front door.

"Oh, sorry." Confused, she gazed up. Who would be standing on the other side of her front door without knocking? Her heart wedged itself in her throat, constricting her ability to breathe. "Noah? Why are you here?"

A sad, yet hesitant expression crossed his face. "I came to make sure you made it home with your rental car and to apologize for my behavior yesterday."

"Oh." Ruth knew better than to get her hopes up. She sensed Noah still had a lot of things to sort out, but unless he asked, she'd remain silent. "Apology accepted."

In his arms, Houston barked and tried to free himself of Noah's grasp. Noah's dog would make the kids at the hospital laugh with his antics. Ruth petted him on the head as she heard the neighbor's cat growl from underneath the bush. She really wished that beast would take up residence somewhere else. "It's good to see you again, too, buddy."

"I also came by to talk to you." Disappointment flared in his eyes. "But I see you're ready to go somewhere."

Noah's hesitation changed her ability to remain unaffected by his charm. Ruth glanced at her watch. Her stomach flopped worse than if she'd just gotten off a roller coaster. "I'm on my way to a birthday party, but I still have a few minutes. Why don't you come inside for a moment?"

"I don't want to keep you."

Ruth put a hand on his arm to stop him from leaving. "No. I'm here for you, Noah. As a friend. And friends don't let others suffer without trying to help. Please come inside. I can be a little late. The kids are used to my crazy schedule."

"Kids?" Noah followed her inside, Houston leading the way.

She motioned for Noah to sit on her couch while Houston took off to investigate the rest of her house. She took the seat opposite the coffee table on the matching oversized toffee-colored love seat, glad she'd had the foresight to straighten the room after she'd wrapped her gift. "Not my own kids. I'm a volunteer over at the Children's Center in the hospital. It's Marissa's birthday today, and we're throwing her a party."

"It's not right that kids have to spend their birthday in a hospital."

To keep her hands busy, Ruth reached in her knitting basket and pulled out her really bad scarf. It looked no better than her other knitting project she kept in her duffel bag for the plane rides, but the click of the needles brought her a measure of comfort.

"There's a lot of things that aren't right or fair. But I try to make things better for those less fortunate. I love making those kids happy. Too bad I can't say I love this." She held up the uneven pink and purple long rectangular scarf.

"My mom's taken up knitting, too. I hate to admit it, but she's not much better than you. Please tell me you're not actually going to make someone wear that thing?"

Ruth grinned at Noah. There was no way she'd send this monstrosity to her niece back in Wisconsin. She'd probably unravel it and start over again. "Sure. Come here, Houston. Here boy."

Houston's long nails clicked against the tile floor when he skittered to a stop. Ruth wound the scarf, needles and all, around his neck. "There. I think he likes it."

Houston's ears perked up and his tongue hung from his

panting mouth as his attention bobbed between them. Noah's chuckle joined hers. "Please take it off."

"I know. It's really awful. So how many awful things did your mom make you?"

Noah stilled for a moment, his expression growing somber. Ruth had crossed some invisible line, and she didn't know how to take her words back even if she knew what it was.

"Not me. Jeremy."

Silence lingered between them as Ruth unwound the scarf from Houston's neck and set it back in the basket. This was the first time Noah had mentioned Jeremy. She could feel Noah's pain as if it were her own. The agony of burying a child could bring even the proudest man or woman to their knees. Her parents had managed to keep things together because of their faith, and they had other children who needed them. Noah had no one. He also didn't have any faith, and until he was willing to accept Him into his life, things wouldn't change.

Sunlight filtered in through the open blinds and cast striped shadows across the distressed wood coffee table. On instinct, Ruth moved to sit next to Noah. She wound her arm through his and briefly rested her head on his shoulder. "I'm so sorry about your wife and son."

A hesitant spark troubled Noah's gaze. "Michelle was pregnant when she died."

His mouth opened and then closed. He still needed to talk about whatever bothered him, but his pride stood in the way. What would it take for him to open up so she could help him?

"I'm very sorry about that, too." Oh, Noah. He'd lost even more than she'd realized. Her voice softened and she stared up at Noah, willing him to speak what was on his mind. He needed to let go of the dark cloud hovering over him and talk more about his wife and son. But only when he was ready. His face filled her vision. Forget the friendship. In that instant, Ruth found herself falling in love. "I suspect you didn't come back here to talk about our childhoods. What *did* you want to talk about, Noah?"

Noah stood, dislodging a disgruntled Houston. "It can wait. I'm sure you have to go."

Ruth glanced at her watch again, surprised at how much time Noah's visit had eaten. And yet, nothing had been resolved. Noah looked more troubled than when he'd walked through her front door. "It can't wait. Come with me today. The kids will love Houston, and when you're ready, we'll take a break in the cafeteria and talk there."

"Hi, Marissa. Happy birthday, honey." Ruth enfolded the tiny girl in her arms as soon as Ruth entered the playroom.

Within seconds, the group of kids swallowed Ruth in their midst, leaving Noah with an excited Houston squirming in his arms standing on the fringes. He wasn't so sure about this. Agreeing to come to the birthday party at the hospital was one thing, but he wasn't prepared to deal with the memories it brought to the surface. His gaze skimmed the brightly painted park scene on the walls as his feet planted themselves on the dark green carpet. While the room contrasted against the stark white one where his son had died, the underlying smell of death and antiseptic remained.

He tightened his grip on Houston. Definitely not a good idea.

"Miss Ruthie, you made it." The olive-skinned girl grinned and threw her arms around Ruth's neck. "I knew you would. I just knew it."

Noah watched Ruth settle herself on her knees in the

midst of the children. On their level. Talking with them, not at them. Obviously, Ruth was more than just a volunteer in here. Another contradiction. Her sunny smile as she interacted with the sick children almost made him forget. Almost. But in the back of his mind, he remembered. Noah also remembered that he needed to talk to Ruth about Hannah's illness.

"Of course I did. I wouldn't miss your party for all the chocolate in the world." Ruth pulled the skinny arms from around her neck. "And I've brought a special visitor today to help celebrate."

Ruth stood and held out her hand to Noah. "Kids, I'd like you to meet Mr. Barton and his dog, Houston. Everyone say hello."

"Hello, Mr. Barton. Houston." A chorus of young voices answered as they welcomed him into their midst. Many hands reached out to pet his dog. Houston loved all the attention and tried to gain his freedom so he could play with all the children.

Noah tried to catch Ruth's eye to see if he should put the dog on the carpet, but she was too caught up in listening to a story from one the young boys holding her hand. He glanced around the room, looking for an authority figure, but only came up with several smiling parents, and his elderly neighbor, Mrs. Murphy, cradling a young toddler in her arms. Was Mrs. Murphy a volunteer like Ruth or was the little girl her grandchild?

An uncomfortable weight settled across his heart. In the few brief conversations he'd had with the woman, the subject of family had never come up. He'd preferred it that way because then he wouldn't have to get involved. He stared at the top of Ruth's head again, among all the different shades of color from blond to red to black.

How had he allowed himself to become so selfish? Bile rose in his throat. He used to care. He had a reason to care.

"May I pet your dog?"

Noah angled his head to stare down at a small, solemn girl. Her long dark hair had been pulled to the sides in pigtails and tied with matching purple ribbons. Her big blue eyes gazed up at him in a disconcerting way before the girl's attention swiveled to the tall brunette woman with the stylish short hair wearing scrubs that approached to his left. The girl's face broke into a smile. "Mama, you're here."

"Of course, pumpkin. I snuck away for a few minutes to join in the fun." The woman got on her knees and hugged her daughter before holding her at arm's length. Then she straightened one of the ribbons and adjusted her hair. "How are you feeling today?"

"A little sleepy, but okay. I want to pet the dog though. Am I allowed?" The girl turned back to Noah. "Please?"

"I don't see why not as long as it's okay with his owner."

The girl's paleness contrasted with the woman's lightly tanned skin. He also realized the carefully tended hair bound in pigtails was really a wig. Where was the child's hair? No child should have to go through this. Noah's heart continued to ache. He'd always known there were sick children in the world, but outside of Jeremy's accident, he'd never had any experience with them. He'd always thought of them as nothing more than a face in a photograph. A flat image instead of a living, breathing person. Standing in this little girl's presence gnawed at his selfishness.

Noah squatted like Ruth had done with the other children so he could be at eye level with the child. "Of course. Better yet, would you like to hold Houston?"

The girl nodded and held out her skinny arms. Her solemn expression disappeared again with a lick from Houston. Her giggles filled the cramped space between them. "Houston, you're cute. Mama, can we get a dog when I get better?"

Noah stood again and watched the interaction between mother and child with interest. The uncertainty unnerved him. So did the woman's obvious pain.

"Of course, pumpkin. When you get better. I'm Dr. Kennedy." The woman held out her hand. "That's my daughter, Kendall."

"Noah Barton. Pleased to meet you. And Houston, of course." Noah wondered what type of medicine she practiced.

"He's such a cute dog. I haven't seen my daughter react so positively in a while. Thanks for bringing him today." Dr. Kennedy's eyes misted, contradicting the strong woman he sensed she portrayed to the world.

"It wasn't my idea. It was Ruth's." Noah almost put his arm around Ruth's waist when she joined them. He stopped just in time. They weren't a couple. Far from it. Because that would mean he'd have to care again. Put his heart out there. He just wasn't ready. But the whole "friends" thing wasn't working right now.

"Hi, Adrienne. It's good to see you again. I just wish it wasn't under these circumstances." Ruth hugged the taller woman.

"Hi, Ruth. I know. This remission was shorter than the last. I'm at my wit's end."

"I'll be there for you. Just let me know what I can do."

"The dog was a start. Thanks. She's happier than I've seen her since the new diagnosis. I just wish I had the time and energy to adopt one for home." A frown crested the doctor's forehead as she glanced at her watch. "I've only got a few more minutes left. I'd like to spend them with Kendall, if you don't mind."

"Not at all."

After the doctor joined her daughter, and Houston was passed around between the children, Noah thrust his hands through his hair. God had obviously forsaken and abandoned these kids, too, by allowing the sickness and death. He didn't care about them any more than He'd cared about Jeremy. Heaviness descended.

Noah's fingers itched to caress Houston's fur and feel his warmth, yet he couldn't rip his dog from the arms of the children who obviously needed him.

"I really want to thank you for coming today. The kids are all in love with Houston. He's really made their day." Ruth stopped speaking. Her brow furrowed and concern flashed in her expressive green eyes. "I'm so sorry. I wasn't thinking. This must be too hard for you. Let me grab Houston so you can leave."

"And miss the cake and presents? I'm fine. Really. What's wrong with Kendall?" But Noah wasn't fine. Far from it.

"Leukemia. What upsets Adrienne the most is she's a pediatric doctor, yet she can't help her own child."

Noah's lips pursed. He knew the feeling. The helplessness. The hopelessness. He'd stood vigil over his son's hospital bed for two days. He'd prayed, he begged, he'd even threatened the Lord, but his son had been taken from him anyway. His fingers curled. He would not wish that on any one of the parents or grandparents in this room. "Can't they do a bone marrow transplant?"

Ruth placed a hand on his arm. Even the warmth of her skin couldn't chase away the cold seeping into his pores. "They haven't found a match yet. And the chemo doesn't look like it's helping this time around, either."

"What about the rest of them?"

"Our birthday girl, Marissa, is waiting for a heart. Every day she's with us remains a blessing. Carlos, the little Hispanic boy by the bookshelves with the curly brown hair, has an autoimmune disorder. Jacob is recovering from another round of skin grafts, and the girl holding Houston right now, Gabby, is waiting for a kidney."

Cancer? Burn victims? Transplants? Noah cringed. Especially at his last thought. Some of these patients and Hannah faced the same issue. How could God turn His back on his office manager and these innocent children?

The sound of laughter and barking erupted in the room as a staff member dressed as a clown wearing big blue shoes stumbled into the play area with a large bunch of multicolored balloons. The person underneath the silly costume honked a long bicycle horn, which made Houston growl and bark even louder, much to the delight of the children.

Noah's neighbor waved at him when their gazes met. He waved back. "What about the woman with the child in her arms in the rocking chair?"

"Mrs. Murphy's granddaughter has AIDS. Her mother was a drug-addicted prostitute who's serving time in prison right now."

The emotion in Ruth's voice and in her expression made his stomach churn. Sweat formed across his brow and under his arms. Breathing became difficult. He should get out of here, but his feet stayed planted to the carpet, almost as if they'd attached themselves to the fiber.

Ruth must have sensed his distress again. She wound her arm through his, her voice low and soothing. "This is too difficult for you. Please help yourself to a cup of coffee in the cafeteria. I'll be down shortly."

The shrill of Noah's cell phone saved him from a response. He didn't even really know why he was here anymore. Glad for the diversion, Noah flipped his phone open and answered. "Noah Barton speaking."

After Ruth released her hold, Noah backed up so he could lean against the wall. He couldn't shake the feelings inside him that she evoked. He should go, but he continued to watch her as he listened to the person from the alarm company on the other end of the line.

He shouldn't stare.

His mother hadn't raised him to be rude, but he couldn't help himself. The more he learned about this woman, the more he wanted to throw the whole friendship thing out the window, and ask for more. "I'll be right over to check things out. Thanks." He flipped his phone shut.

"Ruth, the alarm is going off in my office. I need to go check it out."

"Of course you do. Let me grab Houston for you."

"No, wait." One look at Houston belly-up on the floor, the center of attention with a group of children, and Noah knew his dog wasn't going anywhere any time soon. Desolation washed over him. He and Houston rarely spent time apart. They were a team. Noah finally understood now that he'd used Houston as a security blanket to keep his loneliness at bay, and that wasn't helping either one of them.

"Houston can stay if you don't mind watching him. I'll be back in a bit." Before he left, Noah reached in his pocket and retrieved a quarter. Then he walked over and squatted in front of the birthday girl and pretended to pull it out from behind her right ear. He placed it in her hand. "Happy birthday, Marissa."

The little girl squealed and bounced around like Jeremy used to.

Pain wrapped around his heart. He'd forgotten how soft and funny children could be. Noah squeezed his eyes closed to shut out the image, but Jeremy's features superimposed themselves on Marissa's face. His fingers curled into tight fists. When would all the grief and the guilt go away? When would his life start to mean something again? When would he forget that the woman he wanted to consider more than a friend also served as a constant reminder to what he'd lost?

After the cake and presents and with Houston still the hit of the party, Ruth felt comfortable enough to leave him with the children for a few minutes so she could grab a cup of coffee. On her way back from the staff vending machine, she found her good friend Samantha Riedle at the nurses' station with her own cup of coffee.

Marissa and her mother walked down the hall toward the play area again after a quick visit to her hospital room, the little girl dressed in a new fairy costume and carrying her new doll with the matching outfit that had been Ruth's present. Her plastic heels clicked on the tile floor as her laughter filled the silence.

"Look, Miss Samantha. Isn't Miss Ruth the best?" Marissa twirled around in a swirl of pink, purple and blue fabric.

"She sure is, sweetheart." Samantha dropped a packet of the blue sweetener into her cup. "Don't ever forget it. Either of you."

Marissa's crown slipped, but Ruth reset it upon the little girl's head before she pranced down the hall, her mother in tow. Then Ruth's gaze skimmed across the empty space in front of the elevator. Even though she'd seen Noah leave, she could still feel his presence inside the hospital. Leaning against the chest-high counter, she couldn't decide if that was a good thing or not as she propped her chin on a fisted palm.

She liked him—no, more than liked him. She loved him more than a friend should.

Her friend blew on the black beverage and eyed Ruth over the rim of her "Have A Heart" mug. "So who's the man?" Samantha reached out and placed her hand on Ruth's forearm.

Ruth lifted her head, clutched the edge of the nurse's station counter and stared at her cup.

"A friend. Noah Barton. He's one of the pilots for that new company AeroFlight contracted with." Ruth whispered.

"Just a friend? Right. Does he make you happy?"

"I don't know. He makes me feel a lot of things since David—"

"Don't even think of bringing that old boyfriend of yours into this. Sometimes I think you use David as an excuse to keep from getting involved with someone else. You're attracted to him. I can see it in your eyes. So what's up?"

"Noah's uncomfortable with my beliefs, he doesn't like my job, and…" She breathed in what was supposed to be a calming breath, yet the oxygen filling her lungs did little to soothe the butterflies.

"And what? He doesn't like kids? He's married?" Samantha traced the red heart on the cup.

The clock on the opposite wall ticked off the seconds. The gnawing in her stomach intensified. Noah had done a great job with the kids under the circumstances until the end when she'd sensed his need to escape. His visit today meant that maybe—just maybe—he was starting to come around to them. To her job. But that wasn't what made her so unsure. Noah's expression at the cemetery still haunted her. "He's still in love with his dead wife. I can't compete with that."

Chapter Nine

"I still say dinner isn't necessary." Noah held open the restaurant's door twenty minutes after dropping Houston off at his condo.

"And I say it is," Ruth replied as she stepped through the threshold. "Think of it as a thank-you for making the kids so happy. Nothing more."

He didn't know why he even agreed to come. Was it an unconscious ulterior motive to try to make his life seem more normal? Or did he really want a conversation with someone who could actually speak something other than canine? At least he'd had the presence of mind to suggest here instead of the hospital cafeteria.

He stopped short of running into her when she turned to face him. All resistance fled as her expressive green eyes looked up at him and her voice softened to a whisper. "Both you and Houston did a wonderful job with the children today. I really appreciate that and so did the staff and parents."

"It was nothing." Noah wanted to say more as they squeezed together on a bench in a spot meant for one while waiting for a table, but his lips refused to form any coherent words. He eyed the fire marshall's occupancy sign hung near the cash register. Manny's Diner had pretty much exceeded that limit, but that wasn't what made him squirm.

"Hi, Noah." A harried server scrambled by with her arms full of dirty dishes. "Sorry for the wait. They crawled out of the woodwork today."

"No problem, Lourdes. Glad to see business is good." He didn't miss the petite Hispanic woman's glance at Ruth or the server's raised eyebrows and devious grin. It scared Noah. He was afraid to let go and fall in love again. What if he lost her, too?

Unable to see more than the crown of Ruth's blond head and the way her fingers had curled around the top of her tan purse, his gaze skimmed the donkey pulling the cart painted on the white wall opposite them. Then it slipped past the silk plants stationed in the corners and over the colorful tiled tables and leather chairs filled with customers. Eventually it wandered back to the woman next to him. He was getting used to this sense of companionship.

"Come here often?" Ruth's throaty voice hinted of amusement at the corny pickup line when she caught his attention on her.

"As often as I can. Cooking for one has never appealed to me."

"I know the feeling. It must be pretty good to still have a wait at three-fifteen in the afternoon."

The couple beside them vacated the bench, and Ruth slid over, as if glad to have some breathing room. Her action relieved and disappointed him, though he could now settle back and set his foot over his knee.

"It is. Especially the sampler platter, which is what I

suggest." He stretched his arm across the back of the bench. With a slight adjustment, he could wrap it around her shoulder as if they were a couple.

Which they weren't. They were just friends. If his head managed to convince his heart.

"Noah, your table is ready." The hostess, Maria, grabbed some menus before she led them into the interior of the restaurant.

Noah stood, helped Ruth to her feet and escorted her into the dining area. He refused to be affected by her soft skin. It was easier for his brain to issue the command then for his body to obey it. Her fragrance engulfed him again. An intangible emotion grabbed his heart and refused to let go. He cared.

"Here you go." Maria set the menus on a cozy table near the back.

"You can let go now." Ruth's breathless voice held him spellbound.

"Right." Grudgingly, Noah released her, noting the rapid pulse beating at the base of her neck and the slow flush that crept in and bloomed in her cheeks. Did all blondes blush so easily or simply the one holding his interest a little bit more than his comfort zone allowed?

He held out the chair for Ruth before he took his own seat across from her. "Duncher," the combination between lunch and dinner as Jeremy used to call it, had been a bad idea. But he needed to talk to her about Hannah. He'd just have to put his emotions aside. But with those feelings cut off for more than three years, starting the conversation about his office manager was like trying to get an infant to fly a plane.

Once she regained her equilibrium, Ruth liked the quaint Mexican restaurant. Fresh cut flowers on the colorful tiled tables put her at ease, despite the crowd. So did the murals on the walls depicting rural Mexican life. She eyed the basket of chips and salsa after the busboy dropped them off. The aroma made her stomach growl. Despite the cake and ice cream at the hospital, she was hungry.

"Hi, Noah. The usual?" The waitress who had spoken to them earlier flipped open her order pad.

"Yes. And an order of nachos. That should take care of both of us." Noah handed the menus back to Lourdes, but his attention strayed to Ruth. "I hope you don't mind."

"Not at all." Ruth broke the chip and wedged the bigger piece of it into her mouth. Noah's subdued mood bothered her. She'd made a mistake in inviting him to Marissa's birthday party. In her quest to make the hospital a happier place for the kids, she hadn't thought of what it would do to Noah. Especially since he'd lost his son at such a young age. Her fingers strangled the cloth napkin in her lap. "So what *is* the usual?"

"A sampler platter of different food."

"Oh, that sounds great. Thanks for ordering." She exhaled slowly, appreciating that she didn't have to decipher the menu. "So have you lived in the valley all your life?" She finally asked, trying to start the conversation and find out what really bothered him and why he'd come by her house today.

"Long enough."

More silence surrounded them until the customers at the table next to them left in a flurry of activity. Ruth broke apart another chip and placed it in her mouth. The slightly greasy, salty corn chip delighted her taste buds, but getting Noah to talk proved a bigger challenge than making sure her older brother remembered their parents' anniversary.

She tried to reach out to Noah again.

"So I take it you're from somewhere else, like a lot of the people here." She ran her finger along the condensation on the water glass and tilted her gaze at him.

"I grew up in Chicago." His long, lean fingers stiffened around his coffee cup. "We moved here when I was flying for Southern Skies Airlines."

Ruth knew enough about body language to know that talking about his former job was part of the source of his problem. Were his wife and son killed in an airplane crash? Or did their deaths occur while Noah was flying? Attuned to his distress, she reached across the brightly tiled table to place her hand on his and changed the subject. "We were practically neighbors then. I grew up outside of Milwaukee. Do you miss the Midwest?"

He eyed her hand yet didn't pull away. His other hand crept over hers. "Not really, though I do miss a white Christmas every once in a while."

Ruth smiled, liking the feel of his touch. "I know what you mean. Snow on Christmas seemed like a prerequisite in our house. My mom used to send all of us outside to build the biggest snowman ever to keep us from underfoot while she prepared the family feast. My oldest brother was notorious for helping himself to the main course before it made it to the table. The first few years here were hard, but I'm used to it now. Especially when I hear about a blizzard up there. I can't take the cold anymore."

"Likewise. If I'm not flying somewhere on the holidays, I'm out on my ATV."

"That sounds like fun." *I hope you wear a helmet.* Pulling her hand from his to give the waitress room to put their appetizers down along with two empty plates, she frowned. She'd seen too many casualties from motorcyclists and ATV enthusiasts who didn't wear helmets. Several of them became organ donors.

"It is. You should try it with me sometime. I have an extra helmet." He gazed at her, the question in his eyes mingled with caution before he turned his attention to the woman standing next to the table. "Thanks."

"And here's your extra hot sauce." She placed a white bowl on the table with a dark red puree in it. "Do you need anything else?"

They both shook their heads.

"Enjoy. I'll check back a little later." Then she disappeared back into the kitchen.

When Ruth settled herself in and bowed her head, she heard Noah shift in his chair. She sensed his discomfort, yet her lips moved in silence as she offered a prayer for her meal—and Noah.

Ruth eyed the pile of food in the middle of the table. The nachos covered with lots of melted cheese looked yummy. She should have asked what the sampler platter included. While she recognized the mini tacos, not much else looked familiar. There was no way she could eat all this food. She and Noah could have shared one appetizer and still had leftovers. Still staring at the plate, Ruth couldn't figure out where to begin.

"Is there a problem?" Noah asked, reaching for the hot bowl of salsa.

"Not really, though if you could help identify what's on the plate, it would be helpful."

He raised his eyebrows. "You don't eat Mexican food? I should have thought to ask. I'm sure they make some type of gringo food, even if it's for kids."

"I'm fine, Noah. I'm partial to Italian food, but I'm always eager to try new things."

"Why didn't you say so? There's a great Italian restaurant not too far from here. Next time."

Next time? Hope sprang inside her heart.

Noah used his fork as a pointer. "Two shredded beef mini tacos, a pollo fundido, which is basically a chicken chimi with a cream sauce, a bean tostada, a cheese enchilada and two chicken taquitos."

He pulled half of the fundido from the plate and served it to Ruth before he took the other half and one of the tacos. His thoughtfulness made her squirm. So used to helping other people, this whole thing about Noah waiting on her made him all the more attractive. She found herself liking the idea and him despite the alarms going off inside her brain.

"I guess you don't want any of this hot sauce then?" Noah winked. His word touched on the amused side as he held up the bowl of red puree.

"No, thanks. I like my food on the milder side."

"Maybe we could change that, because sometimes a little spice can add a new dimension." Noah poured the hot salsa all over his food.

"Or cause heartburn." Ruth grinned and felt a different heat burn her cheeks.

She took a few bites of her chicken and let the flavors burst across her tongue. "This isn't too bad. I must have carried out from the wrong restaurants when I moved to Tucson."

"What made you move there from Milwaukee?" Noah asked before he bit into his mini taco.

"I attended the nursing school at the University of Arizona."

"That's a long way from home. Why? There's got to be other schools a lot closer."

Ruth remained silent for a moment. "I followed someone. Things didn't work out, but I stayed, anyway."

Digging her fork into the small pile of refried beans that Noah had also put on her plate, she twisted the utensil around. She'd met her first serious boyfriend at a church camp in Texas. He had attended U of A so Ruth had decided she needed to also. Having led a pretty sheltered life, her limited experience hadn't prepared her for his lies or his lack of true faith. And then there was the commitment-shy David. Her track record with men wasn't impressive. She glanced up at an intent Noah staring at her. Was her heart leading her down another path of disaster?

"I'm sorry to hear that, but glad that you're here." Noah sounded like he meant it, but she couldn't be sure.

"It's okay. I'm over it." But she wasn't. Not really. Her track record clouded her perception of men and made her wary. Made her unavailable. Made her hide behind her job, the kids at the hospital and pints of Ben & Jerry's because fairy tales didn't exist.

Ruth shrugged off her disappointment over some of the curveballs God had thrown at her. The old, familiar phrase echoed in her mind. *The will of God will never take you where the grace of God will not protect you.* He'd protected her then and would continue to do so, whatever He had in mind for her.

Noah dropped a cheese-covered chip when he went to place some nachos on her plate. His fingers accidentally brushed hers when they both tried to retrieve the wayward food, but instead of grabbing the chip, he held on to her hand, looking a tad bit uncomfortable. "Ruth, are you seeing someone?"

She stilled as more hope blossomed inside. "No. Not at the moment."

Ruth held her breath.

"Good. Me, either. So neither one of us needs to worry

about someone getting jealous because we ate together. As friends."

And for a brief moment, Ruth had thought he might be interested in her as she exhaled her disappointment. But then she thought of his late wife and how he couldn't let go; she knew otherwise. Still, regret curbed her hunger, and the mouthful of food she just swallowed tasted like a cotton swab. "No. You don't have to worry about that on my end." She quickly changed the subject. "So what about you? Where did you go to school?"

"Northern Illinois University in DeKalb." Noah dabbed the paper napkin to his lips. "I didn't stray too far from home until after college. But at least as a pilot, I could visit almost any time I wanted to since my route was primarily the Midwest. Sometimes I wonder what my life would be like or where'd I'd be if I'd attended school somewhere else."

"I know what you mean." Ruth took another bite of chicken and mulled over Noah's words. Even though God was in control, she believed He sometimes let His children wander a bit before guiding them to their ultimate purpose.

"Now that I think about it, I'm actually surprised my overprotective parents let me leave the state." A chill permeated her heated skin. Ruth tried to exorcise the helplessness she'd always experienced around her family by putting food into her mouth. She could get used to eating Mexican food. Or maybe it was the company.

"Overprotective? Why is that?"

"Because my twin sister died when we were eight. My parents were afraid I would, too." Which was why she'd attended school as far away from home as possible. And why she had such limited experience with men and had a bad feeling she was making another mistake.

"Are you?"

"Am I what?"

Noah's mouth opened and shut. Alarm crept into all the angles and planes of his face as he struggled to get the words out. "Are you going to die?"

Ruth fell into the liquid pools of his eyes and understood his fear. He'd already lost his wife and son. He didn't want to lose anyone else. She reached across the small table as if to stroke his cheek, but her hand fell back to the tile. "No. I'm not going to die. At least not from the same thing that my sister did. Rachel had a defective heart."

"I'm really sorry about your sister." Sorrow clogged his voice, and she knew he understood her pain. "That's why you do what you do, isn't it?"

His fingers tenderly pushed a loose curl behind her ear. He stroked the end of her hair as if memorizing every detail. If she stood and leaned a little closer, she could reach his lips.

If she wanted to. And she did.

Ruth nodded, dispelling her sadness and her attraction to Noah. Grabbing her water, she put the cup to her lips to keep from spilling any more words. This whole dinner thing was supposed to be about answering Noah's questions, not about her.

With her stomach full, Ruth pushed her plate away and signaled for a carryout box from the busboy carrying a large tray of dirty dishes back to the kitchen. Then she eyed Noah from beneath her lashes. The man was too good-looking for her comfort. His cropped hair suited him, his crow's feet made him distinguished and the color of his eyes made her think of the lake near her childhood home. Deep and mysterious, with a splash of fun on a hot summer day.

"So Noah, why did you stop by my house earlier?"

Noah shifted on the hard wood chair and stared at the mound of lettuce and tomatoes and a few clumps of shredded cheese he'd left on his plate. He placed his napkin over the remains and gave them a proper burial. "I—I…"

He grabbed a chip and crumbled it between his fingers as the hostess seated another couple at the next table. He dusted the fragments away. Deciding to talk to Ruth this morning after he'd seen Hannah and Dylan had seemed so easy. Actually doing it was harder than he'd expected. Despite the air-conditioning, he felt warm and clammy. The interior of the restaurant seemed to shrink to the size of his hall closest, and he pulled at the collar of his polo shirt in order to breathe.

"Thank you. May I have some coffee, please?" Ruth smiled at the busboy who'd just dropped off a box for her leftovers. Then she turned her attention on him and pressed on. "I'm here for you, Noah. Please share with me what's bothering you."

Her words eased a bit of his anxiety. She made talking about Hannah sound easy.

"My office manager has polycystic kidney disease."

"Oh, Noah. I'm so sorry. How can I help? What do you need to know? Would you like me to talk to her?" Ruth's concern touched him.

How like her to immediately offer assistance to Hannah, a complete stranger. Noah struggled with a reply, but the words caught against his throat. Finally, he nodded to another hovering busboy to remove their plates. Maybe in the interim he could think of something coherent to say.

"There is one thing." The words sounded foreign and unused. "Will you say a prayer for her? I don't seem to be able to."

"Of course." Ruth bowed her head and clutched Noah's hand in hers. "God, please keep Noah's office manager in Your loving care. Help her to receive the best possible medical care, and heal her body. Amen."

Amen. The word echoed inside Noah's brain.

"How far along is she?"

"End stage."

"End stage?" Concern flared in Ruth's eyes. "She doesn't have a lot of options." Ruth's compassion surrounded him like a comforting blanket as she squeezed his arm. He could get used to the feeling again. Yes, he had his dog, but he missed the human touch and the closeness.

"I know. She's scheduled to have her kidneys removed next week."

"She can go on dialysis."

"Not what she wants to do. She wants a new kidney." His harsh words matched his emotions. Putting it out there meant he couldn't keep his secret any longer. Not that he wanted to anymore. Sharing Hannah's health problems with Ruth meant he was ready for the next step. Ready to move on. Ready to accept what happened. Ready to help Hannah in whatever way he could.

"Here you go." Lourdes dropped off two cups of steaming black coffee, some containers of cream, and a bowl full of sugar and sugar substitute packages. "I figured you'd like some, too, Noah. Just like always."

"Thanks."

Silence deafened the distance between them as Ruth dumped two containers of cream and a packet of pink sweetener in her cup. The click of the spoon against the side grated on his nerves a bit. Ruth's eyes softened to the color of freshly mown lawn. "Noah, please tell me if I'm out of line, but were Michelle and Jeremy organ donors?"

"Jeremy was." Noah drew out the words.

Ruth bowed her head for a moment before making eye contact with him again. He saw the understanding dawn in her expression, and she reached across the table to squeeze his arm again. "Nobody explained anything to you, did they? That's why this is so hard for you."

"No. All that woman wanted was to pass his organs around like a Thanksgiving turkey."

"I have a feeling I know who you're talking about. She's no longer working in that area anymore. Not that it will make you feel any better."

"Not really." At least she didn't thank him or give him the mumbo jumbo line about how his son's organs had helped other people. Her sensitivity to his feelings left him raw and at the same time thankful she'd left his dignity intact, and it made him care about her more than he should, even though he wasn't ready for anything more.

"I'll help you understand this the best that I can," Ruth continued. She stood and moved her chair around to the other side of the table kitty-corner from him but still remained out of the way of the servers. She took a sip of her coffee before placing her hand on his again. "There is one other option. She can have what's called a live transplant."

Noah liked the words better already. He also liked the way the soft overhead lighting picked up the slight reddish tints in her hair and the way the warmth of her hand felt against his skin. "A live transplant?"

"That's where a living person donates a kidney to the one in need. They do both surgeries at once. Transplants tend to be a little more successful and last longer through this option because the donor is living. They just did a multiple surgery like this a few months back, and everyone is doing great."

"You can live with one kidney?"

"Of course. For some reason God gave us a spare." Ruth's voice dropped to a whisper. "I can test to see if I'm a match. So can you."

"You would do that?"

"I would. I have before. I just have never been a match." Her gaze dropped from his, and she ran her fingers along the rim of the cup. "Of course, there's the other option we haven't discussed yet. Do you want to hear about it?"

Noah's gut clenched and sweat gathered under his arms.

"No. I mean yes. I wouldn't have brought it up otherwise. I've been thinking of it since I found out yesterday. I know that a deceased donor is the more likely scenario." Noah began to play with the glass salt and pepper shakers, shuttling them around each other. "That's why I've come to you. To find answers. To find hope."

To find love? Impossible.

"Then I'll do the best I can to explain. As you mentioned, a deceased donor is probably the best option. That's where my team or one like it comes in to retrieve the organ and place it in a recipient. What's your office manager's name?" Ruth questioned softly.

Noah took a long sip of coffee before he spoke. Was he crossing a line with his employee by giving out her information even in an attempt to help? He had no choice. He couldn't sit back and do nothing. Hannah's life and Dylan's happiness depended on it. "Hannah Stevenson."

"I'll make some inquiries. I'm assuming she's on the waiting list?"

Noah nodded. The goodness in this woman astounded him.

The trill of Ruth's cell phone shattered the mood.

"Excuse me for a second. I'm on call tonight." Ruth

appeared reluctant as she reached for the BlackBerry attached to her purse and turned slightly away from him. "Ruth Fontaine."

Noah didn't need to hear the person on the other end to know what the call entailed. She was being called out on another coordination. But where was the anger? The denial? The guilt over his son's death? Only a fraction clutched him this time, but it was still there. Waiting. Watching. Not wanting to let go because the guilt had infiltrated every cell in his body.

Ruth disconnected the call and gave him a look of trepidation as she pulled her wallet from her purse. "I'm sorry, Noah. I have to go. I'll keep Hannah in my prayers."

"I understand." Noah put out his hand and stopped her from paying the tab. "Your money's no good here. I'm buying."

"But, it's my treat." Ruth insisted as she placed her purse strap over her shoulder.

"No, it isn't. I insist." Noah retrieved several bills from his wallet and threw them on the table. Then he took the napkin from his lap, set it on the table and pushed his chair away. "Good thing we brought separate cars. Let me walk you to yours."

He wrapped his arm around her waist and walked her through the restaurant and out the front door. She felt so right in his arms. His gaze scraped the cloudless blue sky, and Noah shook his head, confused. Once Ruth sat safely behind the wheel, he suddenly had the urge to jump in next to her and accompany her to the coordination.

Despite what he'd told her in anger, he realized he did want to learn more, and that he wanted to spend a lot more time with her.

Chapter Ten

"Noah? What are you doing here?" A just-woken-from-a-deep-sleep Ruth answered her front door Sunday morning. Her eyes widened, and her body tried to catch up with what her brain had already recognized. She stared at Noah and Houston, or rather Houston's shaggy back end as he sniffed under the tree, trying to find her neighbor's cat.

She came around instantly and stared down at her bare feet. At least she was dressed. Kind of. If she counted the clothes she'd worn yesterday as dressed. She must have literally fallen into bed this morning, which meant she hadn't brushed her teeth or combed her hair. Heat flushed her cheeks as she pressed her fingers to her lips. Yet Noah didn't seem to notice.

"It's not exactly morning. It's five past noon." And Noah looked every inch ready to face the day with his light blue polo shirt and khaki shorts. The noon sunlight glinted off his damp dark hair, and the light scent of aftershave wafted by her nose.

"Five past what? I slept through church?" Ruth groaned.

"I've even missed the late service. I never miss church unless I'm out on a call. I must have forgotten to set the alarm." Though she had to admit, being awakened by Noah left her heart beating faster and her lungs fighting to take in oxygen.

"You probably needed the sleep and I'm sure the—" Noah hesitated for a moment and pulled his collar "—the Lord won't mind you missing a service or two occasionally. What time did you get in last night?"

At Noah's mention of God, hope blossomed in her heart. Maybe he'd begun to make his peace. She just continued to pray he would and that she'd be there to help him if needed. "Three a.m."

"That's late." Compassion laced his voice.

"My job knows no boundaries, only opportunities." Pride tangled with remorse at her words. She had the most handsome man she'd even seen standing on her doorstep, and yet both had issues that still tainted the air between them.

"Let's hope one of those opportunities is for Hannah." Noah spoke quietly and shifted into the sliver of shade cast by the tiny porch.

"I continue to pray for that. Would you like to come in?" Ruth opened the front door a little wider, and Houston shot in the space between her right leg and the door frame.

"Not right now." Noah held up a large rectangular box. "I came to install some motion lights, but I'll come back later. Will three work?"

Motion lights. To light her way and keep her safe when she dragged in late at night. Ruth should be put off by his overprotectiveness, but she wasn't. He wasn't family. But then again, she suddenly realized that her parents and siblings had only wanted what they thought best for her, too, because they loved her. Did Noah love her even when they'd both agreed on friendship?

Ruth ran a hand through her unbound curls. "Look, Noah. I don't want to inconvenience you. You're here. You may as well stay and put them in."

"Are you sure?" His expression changed as if he'd just noticed her state of dress. Crimson stained his neck and took residence on his face. "Look. I ran out of coffee this morning and could use another cup. Would you like me to get you one while I'm at it?"

How sweet.

"I'd appreciate that. Thanks." She rubbed her eyes against the light filtering in from behind Noah. Not only was he bringing back a decent cup of coffee but he was also giving her time to shower and change.

"There's a good place that's not too far. I'll be back in twenty minutes. Come on, Houston."

Ruth blushed when his gaze lingered on her lips.

For a moment, the cozy sense of a brief companionship lingered in the air around them until Noah quickly departed.

While he was gone Ruth showered and tried to force her hair into a twist. Not happening. She gave up and forced a headband on as her doorbell echoed through the house.

This time when she opened the door ready to face the day, Noah held out the cup of coffee with two little containers of cream and a few pink packets piled on top. "Here. It's black. I didn't know how much to put in."

"Thanks. I'll fix it up inside." Noah's thoughtfulness at remembering what she put in her coffee jolted her senses awake far more than the caffeine in the liquid. Their arms brushed when she ushered Noah and Houston into the foyer, sending her determination to keep up the just friends status into a freefall.

Their steps echoed on her hardwood floor in the tiny hallway that spilled into her blue-and-white themed kitchen.

"Would you like some toast?" Ruth set her cup down on the white tiled counter and popped two pieces of bread in the toaster.

"I'm good. Thanks." Noah took a sip from his cup.

As Noah eyed the small interior, Ruth wondered if he would find her country-inspired decorations quaint or outdated? And would that be a good thing or a bad thing?

"Before I start, I need to turn off the electricity. Your fuse box is around back?"

"Yes. Right next to the air-conditioning unit. Give me a second and I'll show you." Ruth dumped the contents of both creamers into her cup and one packet of sweetener. She stirred it as she walked to the back door.

"That's not necessary. I can find it. Besides, your toast is burning."

"Oh." As Noah stepped trough the threshold, Ruth ran to retrieve her slightly crispy pieces of bread and slathered the toast with apricot jelly.

Outside, she heard Noah wrestling with the door to the fuse box as she said a quick prayer.

Then she picked up a piece and took a bite before washing it down with a sip of coffee. What was taking Noah so long? Mindlessly taking another bite, Ruth headed back toward the door as she heard the clang of metal against brick.

"Ouch."

Had Noah hurt himself? Ruth's stomach tied itself in knots. How bad? Was it something she could handle or would he need to go to the doctor?

Seconds later, the light and overhead ceiling fan went off. She scurried outside and met Noah on the porch. "What happened?"

"I cut myself. It's no big deal."

No big deal? Then why did she see blood? Placing her toast and coffee on the glass surface of her patio table, Ruth held out her hand. If Noah was anything like her brothers, he'd probably deny that he needed medical attention even if the cut required stitches. The fact that his hand remained bunched in a fist didn't instill much confidence in his diagnosis either. Her voice softened. "I'm a nurse, remember? Let me determine that."

He pulled his hand away and back over his right shoulder. "All it needs is a bandage."

"Good. Then who better to look than me? The bandages and peroxide are in the bathroom. Come on." Ruth wound her arm through his left one and guided him back into the house. On their way through the kitchen, Ruth grabbed a napkin and wiped the thin trail of blood trickling down his wrist. The cut was deeper than Noah led her to believe. She led him into the tiny light tan room off the main hallway, and as she'd expected, the space felt like it shrunk to the size of a shoe box.

Ruth pulled out a first aid kit and a brown bottle out of her medicine cabinet and set them on the tiled counter. Struggling to maintain a professional appearance, she turned back to face him and tried not to let his closeness affect her nursing abilities. "Okay, Noah. Let me see the cut, please."

Reluctantly, Noah held out his hand.

Very gently, Ruth pried his fingers back and exposed the thin, red line bisecting his palm. Blood had started to coagulate along the edge. Good. She traced the calluses accumulated over the years of hard work, yet she remembered his tenderness when dealing with Houston, her kids at the hospital and even her.

"See? It only needs a bandage." Noah's voice seeped into the stillness of the room.

After turning on the faucet, she tugged his strong, capable hand under the stream of water to clean out the wound. Relief filled her sigh. Thankfully, it wasn't as bad as she'd expected. Still, she opened the bottle of peroxide and poured a little over the cut and watched it bubble and turn white. "When was the last time you had a tetanus shot?"

Noah stiffened. "I don't remember."

"I think you should get one as a precaution." She put a little pressure on the spot with a clean, fresh towel she'd pulled from under the sink to stop any residual bleeding.

Taking care of Noah reminded her of what she'd always wanted in a relationship. Companionship, conversation, with some friendship on the side. Something that probably only existed in the fairy tales she didn't believe in yet desperately wanted to today.

"I'll think about it." Noah shifted away from her.

Striving to maintain a more businesslike atmosphere, Ruth focused on her task. "It's not something you should just think about. I've seen what happens when a person gets blood poisoning. It isn't pretty."

"I'm sure you've seen a lot." Noah took the towel from her and dabbed the remaining moisture from his palm. "See? Not bad at all."

"No. Mostly superficial. We're lucky." Ruth gave him a ghost of a smile and opened the cabinet door. She rummaged through various boxes and pulled out a piece of gauze and some tape. "Since your cut is long, I'm going to cover it with this. Try to keep it dry, okay?"

As she softly wrapped the bandaging around his hand, she eyed Noah from beneath her lashes. Even with a slightly crooked nose, the man was too good-looking for her comfort. His cropped hair suited him, his crow's feet made him distinguished and the blueness of his eyes made her want to dive right in. "So, how did you break your nose?"

A slow blush crept across his features. "Brad did it."

"What? Why?" Ruth stopped wrapping his hand.

"He wasn't too happy I decided to date his cousin even though he'd been the one to introduce us. He didn't think I was good enough for Michelle."

"Brad said that?" An incredulous Ruth stared at the man in front her.

Noah took a moment to respond. "Not in those words exactly, but he came around after I married Michelle. We'd been friends too long to let something like that come between us."

Michelle. His late wife. More regret slid across her shoulders as she suddenly imagined all the lonely, bleak years stretching out ahead of her.

Even though she knew she should concentrate on wrapping his hand, her gaze remained on him. He fit into her home, on her porch and anywhere else she could imagine. Against her better judgment, she'd begun to let him into her heart.

Noah rested against the countertop as Ruth placed the tape on the gauze. Noah didn't know which hurt worse: the sting of the peroxide or the expression on Ruth's face when he'd mentioned Michelle. Letting go wasn't as easy as thinking about it, and he'd unwillingly hurt the woman he considered a friend. If only he could cram those words back into his mouth and start the whole conversation over.

Or better yet, ask the question that had brought him here in the first place.

Almost instinctively, Noah bowed his head. Ruth was

wearing off on him, but he caught himself before he uttered a useless prayer. God wouldn't listen anyway, would He?

Not to someone who abandoned Him.

No. He abandoned Noah, too, so Noah would face this alone. Sweat trickled down Noah's forehead and gathered under his arms. Would understanding the process of the organ donation that Hannah faced allow him to finally accept his son's death so he could have peace? Would it allow him to move on? To love again? Or would it only allow the black shadow surrounding him to triumph over his last bit of sanity?

A glimmer of light and hope burst through his thoughts. Anything would be better than this limbo. His question wasn't going to get any easier the longer he stalled. He spoke quickly, finally able to wrap his tongue around the words he'd never been able to vocalize. "Can you explain the process of organ donation?"

The weight he'd carried around on his shoulders decreased.

Noah had been too distraught when Jeremy had been declared brain-dead to ask the questions then, and afterward, bitterness, guilt and pride kept him from researching the answers. Until he met Ruth and started flying the medical personnel around, he'd obliterated the whole concept from his mind, but not anymore.

"I want to understand. I need to understand. What happens?"

Ruth quit wrapping the first aid tape around his hand. She took so long to answer that he wondered if she'd heard him at all. Noah squeezed his eyes shut to clamp down on the emotions swirling around him.

"What would you like to know?" Ruth cut the tape and

set down the supplies before she placed a reassuring hand on his arm.

"Everything," Noah ground out.

"Okay then. Please stop me if this gets to be too much, okay?"

Noah nodded and opened his eyes. He was ready.

"I get called in after a family services coordinator gets family consent to donate." Ruth's soft voice cocooned him in warmth. Her hand remained on his arm, reminding him everyone needed human contact.

"To coordinate the actual donation." Comprehension seeped into his pores and chased away some guilt. Noah finally recognized the difference between the garish woman who'd handed him the clipboard to sign for Jeremy's organs and the woman who stood next to him. A chunk of anger fell away though he still questioned why He had taken his wife and son.

"That other day for instance. The coordination in Rio Salado City. When I arrived at the hospital, I took over the care of the patient. I went through his chart, filled out paperwork and then offered his organs via DonorNet, which matches donors with recipients. That's why I always carry a laptop with me."

"That makes sense." More guilt dissipated, and he wanted to know more. "So what happens then?"

"Well, in that particular case I had three offers from different hospitals with waiting recipients and coordinated the arrival of the teams coming to retrieve them."

"What would happen in Hannah's instance?" Noah placed his hand on top of hers, which still rested on his arm, and squeezed.

"Hannah's on a waiting list. Her information is listed and when an organ becomes available, they'll check for blood type and other factors. Then calls will go out to people on the list that match the criteria. If Hannah isn't healthy enough to do the transplant, or can't get to the hospital in time, the organ will go to someone who can."

Silence lingered between them.

"What do you suppose are Hannah's odds?"

He watched Ruth's expression freeze as she pulled her hand away and turned to put the tape and scissors away. "I honestly can't tell you. I don't know what her stats are or what the condition of her health is. Only her doctor can decide."

More silence inhabited the bathroom, and Noah suspected Ruth hadn't quite told him everything. At least he now had a starting place though. As he stared at Ruth, his thoughts flew back to that afternoon in the hospital. The woman, the clipboard. His sister's words.

He finally got it. He understood. Michelle would have done the same thing had she lived. And she would have wanted her organs donated had she been eligible. He should be so selfless. He had no doubt Ruth had "organ donor" on the back of her driver's license.

"Thanks." Noah twisted his hand around and stared at Ruth's handiwork. "You do good work. No wonder you were such a good nurse. Now that I'm almost as good as new, we've got lights to put in." Noah strode from the bathroom.

Thirty minutes later, he stared at his handiwork above the garage. At least when Ruth came home late at night, she would have enough light to get inside the house safely from either the garage or the front door. He gazed at the woman who now walked out that same front door carrying two glasses of iced tea. Her smile made his heart beat a little faster, his breath come in short gasps, his mind begin to think about wanting to get to know her even more.

Because against his better judgment, the friends thing wasn't working. He cared for Ruth, and his heart wasn't safe anymore.

"Here you go. Thanks for doing this for me. I really appreciate it." As Ruth handed Noah his glass, their fingers touched and created a tiny spark of hope. Noah was ready to conquer whatever else might be on Ruth's to do list of projects so that he could stay near her vibrancy instead of facing the four walls of his condo with his newly found out information.

"No problem. Glad to help. Anything—" The trill of the cell phone cut off his sentence. The look of puzzlement crossed her face when she glanced at the number.

"Ruth Fontaine." Relief filled her expression at the caller's identity. "Oh, hi Samantha. I didn't recognize the phone number. Well, no, I wasn't planning on it. Not today, why?"

Noah tested the lights to give Ruth her privacy for the phone call, but he could still hear the one-sided conversation. What hadn't she been planning to do? Had he intruded on her again with his questions and delayed her from going somewhere important?

Turning to face Noah with a look of uncertainty, Ruth ran a hand through her hair. He could see the indecision hover on her lips. "Oh, I can't. I've got company right now. Please give him a hug and kiss for me and tell him I don't want to see him back there any time soon. Thanks for letting me know."

"Problem? Another job?"

Ruth shook her head. "No. That was one of the nurses at the Children's Center. Carlos is being sent home today, and he wanted to say goodbye to me. She asked if I could come in and visit with the children for a bit."

"And you're not going?" Ruth's answer surprised him.
"No."

Yet written in her eyes Noah saw the anguish and despair. The fact she'd decided to stay with Noah didn't go unnoticed, and it gladdened and troubled him. He understood Ruth's compassion for her kids. He'd begun to feel it yesterday, too.

No longer willing to just exist in the self-imposed exile since Jeremy's death, Noah wanted to reach out and return to the living. Those kids needed her, and Noah was more than willing to share. "But you have to. You can't disappoint Carlos. Tell you what. We're done here except for the cleanup. After I pack my tools, Houston and I will come with you."

Happiness filled Ruth as she stepped back in beside him. She suspected she was seeing a glimpse of the former Noah, and her heart rejoiced. *Thank you, Lord.* "Of course. Just let me freshen up a bit and lock the house."

"You look beautiful, Ruth." Noah's expression softened the longer he stared at her.

The pads of his fingers traced the contours of her cheek. What if there could be more and she'd finally found the one? The thought scared her into questioning his statement. "Really?"

"Really. Makeup would only hide the inner beauty that shines through. Michelle was like that too, but she insisted on the camouflage anyway."

Disappointment and a tiny bit of jealousy singed every cell in her body. Ruth closed her eyes and turned into the palm of his hand, wanting to savor the moment before the fairy tale ended. She'd fallen for the wrong type of man again.

"I'll drive since you've still got the rental. Any word on your car yet?"

"Nope. Though I don't really think I'll hear any good news. My insurance company said it would take ten days for them to determine it unrecoverable. Let me lock up the house then meet you in the truck."

Silence accompanied them the entire ride to the hospital.

Twenty minutes later, Ruth waved to her friend manning the nurses' station before they walked down the fourth floor hall. Ruth reached over and took Noah's hand in hers, wanting to connect with him. Stupidity on her part, but the damage was already done. The moment passed as soon as they entered the playroom and the children engulfed them, pulling Ruth, Noah and Houston in separate directions.

"Who's the new boy?" When she finally had a moment, Ruth asked one of the other nurses who stopped by to deliver medication. She pointed to the little four- or five-year-old towheaded child sitting by himself in the corner.

"His name's Tommy White." The petite redhead lowered her voice. "His foster family dropped him off when they discovered his medical needs were more than they could handle. He hasn't spoken a word since."

"What type of medical issues does he have?"

"He needs a heart transplant like Marissa." The young nurse tsked as she wrote some notes on various charts. "I just don't understand how the Lord can allow such terrible things to happen to innocent children."

"It's not up to us to understand His intentions. I just pray for everyone and do His will on Earth."

"Well, I'm not sure how long I can continue to work in this area. It's killing me to see them in such pain. I need to find another job that's filled with more hope."

"If I hear of anything, I'll let you know. I'm Ruth Fontaine."

"Maggie Carr. Pleased to meet you." She shook Ruth's hand. "I've got to run to the nurses' station for a moment. I'll see you later."

"It was nice meeting you, too."

Ruth's attention strayed back to Noah, surprised to see him sitting against the wall next to Tommy. With his legs stretched out in front of him and Houston perched on his lap, they were both down on the boy's level as if it were the most natural thing. But then again, Noah had experience with children. Firsthand experience. She remembered how uncomfortable Noah had been only yesterday, and her heart went out to him, hoping this wasn't too much for his emotions again. Tears prickled the back of her eyes. She prayed Noah or Houston would be able to reach out and connect with little Tommy and bring him out of his shell.

She wandered back to the group of children playing Twister in the center of the room; yet she was fully aware of the man talking with the new boy on the floor.

"Hi, buddy. What's your name?" Noah continue to sit on the dark green carpet and rest his back against the wall next to the little blond boy off in the corner by himself.

No reply.

Noah's gaze skimmed the short, chopped hair, past his skinny arms that wrapped around his legs, down to the scratches on his feet that stuck out from underneath the blue and white hospital gown. Unease settled in Noah's gut. Why was the boy here? He didn't look sick.

And why, with all the children in the room, had he felt the need to come talk with this one? Though no longer on the outside looking in, Noah understood the isolation and loneliness. It couldn't be that the boy reminded him of Jeremy. The resemblance stopped at the blond hair.

"I'm Noah, and this is Houston." Noah tried again. He settled his dog more comfortably on his lap and ran his fingers through Houston's curly hair, his gaze skimming the huge bookshelves filled with books and all the toys. The room reminded him of the day care center they'd used occasionally for Jeremy, not a room inside a hospital.

Still no reply from the boy.

Houston whined softly and stared up at Noah as if understanding what Noah was trying to do better than Noah knew himself. Anticipation surged through his dog as Houston stood on hind legs and licked Noah's chin. "Down, dog. I know you want to make a new friend. Let's give it a few more minutes."

Houston whined again.

"Houston likes little boys. Would you like to pet him?"

This time Noah's words got a small reaction from the boy. He turned his head and stared up at Noah and Houston, with big blue eyes, so much like Jeremy's. His faced crumpled into tears.

Instinctively, Noah reached out and placed his arm around the boy's bony frame and gathered him close. Houston jumped from his lap and paced around them as Noah rested his chin on top of the boy's head and closed his eyes. Just feeling the small body against his brought out the father in him, and he longed to wrestle away the demons that caused the boy's pain. He understood the look, the hopelessness in the boy's expression. He'd worn a similar one.

A drop of water landed on the back of his hand. A tear. But was it his own or did it belong to the boy? He cared. Too much. He felt himself shying away from the contact. He couldn't deal with this. What had this innocent child done that God had seemed to turn his back on him? Why didn't God care?

Or maybe He did.

The boy had been brought here to find refuge and care from whatever messed up placed he'd been living in.

Houston pawed at them before his warm, pink tongue licked the moisture from their faces. A tiny sound of laughter emerged. Then the boy reached out to pet Noah's dog. "Nice doggie." The child snuggled further into Noah's arms and wrapped his own around Noah's waist. Stunned, Noah remained motionless. Especially when he noticed both Ruth and the nurse staring at them. They quickly approached from opposite ends of the room with genuine smiles creasing their lips.

"Hi, Tommy. I'm Ms. Maggie. I'm one of the nurses who takes care of you."

"And I'm Ms. Ruth." Ruth sat on the opposite side of the little boy. She placed a hand on Tommy's arm and rubbed it gently. "I come in and read to all the children and play games with them. What's your favorite book?"

Tommy turned his head and hid his face against Noah's chest. Tommy. The name suited the small child. Noah tried to pull his emotions back, but it was too late. He squeezed his arm around Tommy's shoulders and let his joy at being able to express himself run down his cheeks. Thanks to Ruth, he'd come back to life.

"That's okay, Tommy." Ruth continued to rub his arm. "No hurry. Whenever you're ready, we'll be here for you. One of us will always be here for you. Either myself, or Ms. Maggie or any one of the nurses or doctors on the floor."

"Me, too." Over Tommy's head, Noah looked at Ruth. He willed her to look at him, but her gaze fluttered to the little boy in his arms. He missed feeling the connection with her and the way her green eyes softened to the color of shamrocks when she looked at him.

"Plus, I'll be one of the coordinators keeping a look out for a new heart for you. Then you'll be good as new. Marissa's waiting for a heart, too. Would you like me to introduce you?"

Noah recoiled slightly. Tommy needed a new heart? The possibility hadn't even crossed his mind that the boy had such a serious health issue. But then again, most of the children here weren't in for the cold or flu. He rubbed his forehead and stared at the boy now holding Ruth's hand as he trudged across the dark green carpet. He wished he could hold Tommy's other hand and reassure him that everything would be okay.

Something told him that it would.

Still, it was hard to imagine that a complete stranger's heart could beat in another person's body. Or another person's kidney could function inside Hannah and make her whole again. Just as Jeremy's organs helped the people who received them live.

Wiping away the sweat that had gathered on his forehead, Noah leaned back and rested his head against the wall. As he closed his eyes and breathed in several fortifying breaths, his hands stilled on Houston's fur. Each time he exhaled, he found himself letting go. Maybe it was time to finally look at the letters from Jeremy's organ recipients.

When his cell phone rang, Houston jumped off his lap. One look at the number and his adrenaline surged. Aero-Flight. Noah rose to his feet. "Desert Wings Aviation."

He listened to the voice on the other end. "No problem. I've got one available. I'll be at the airport in under thirty minutes."

Disappointment lodged in his heart when he made eye contact with Ruth. It didn't look like she would be the co-ordinator on this fly-out because she remained sitting on the floor amidst several children.

Noah also realized he'd have to wait until tomorrow afternoon to find the letters he'd stored away in order to acquaint himself with the people who had received his son's organs.

Chapter Eleven

"Good morning, Hannah." Noah met his office manager at the door Monday morning and held it open for her. His fingers bit into the hard, metal door. She looked worse than when he'd let her go on Friday. "How are you feeling today?"

The redhead stared up at him in surprise as she crossed the threshold. "Fine, Noah. Or as fine as I can be under the circumstances."

But she didn't look fine. Dark circles punctuated the fatigue in her eyes, and her sallow complexion made her freckles stand out even more. Noah wished he could erase her problems and ease the tension radiating from her body. Maybe he could. His talk with Brad after they'd returned from the recovery last night had certainly been enlightening.

Hannah needed a new kidney right away, and waiting for a deceased donor wasn't her only option. Tension tightened his jaw but he found himself ready to explore another alternative.

A fraction of a smile crested on her lips as she placed

her purse underneath her desk and sat down with a sigh. Too bad her words didn't reflect the truth written in her eyes. Hannah was hurting and scared.

"How's Dylan doing?" Noah leaned on the side of Hannah's desk, making small talk because the words he wanted to say remained stuck in his throat.

Before turning on her computer, she straightened a pile of perfectly aligned papers on her desk and stared up at Noah, eyeing him speculatively. "He's holding up well, thanks. Is there something you needed, Noah?"

Releasing his pent-up breath, Noah nodded. He crossed his arms in front of him and decided not to mince his words. Hannah didn't look well enough to deal with the blinking red light on her phone, much less try and play a guessing game. "I was wondering if I could get your doctor's name and number. There's something I'd like to discuss with him."

Hannah fisted her palms and started to stand. Before she wasted any more energy getting her defenses up, Noah held up his hand. "Hear me out Hannah. Please."

Brad walked through the door, momentarily halting the conversation. One look between Noah and Hannah and Brad slipped behind Hannah and placed his hands possessively on her shoulders. She reached up and clutched his fingers. No matter how much both denied it, Noah suspected something was going on between them.

"Hear him out. I think it might work." Brad massaged her shoulders.

Hannah nodded.

"I'd like to find out if one of my kidneys would be compatible for you." There. It was out. He'd said the words, and the tangible relief he felt became evident in his expression.

"You'd do that for me?" A tear slipped over her bottom lash as she stared at her desk. She rearranged the papers on her desk again, but this time her hands trembled like a leaf in the wind.

"I would."

"So would I," Brad whispered.

Noah walked back into his office and let Brad console a crying Hannah.

Ruth kicked off her shoes before she sank down on the leather chair behind her office desk at the Arizona Organ Donor Network—if the tiny space next to the water cooler qualified as a real office. Her pantry was bigger than this, but since she rarely had to spend much time here, she didn't mind so much.

She preferred being out in the field.

Sighing, she massaged her forehead with one hand as she dug in her purse past a pen, her checkbook, her wallet, her lipstick, a mishmash of old receipts she never remembered to file and a hair tie. No bottle of pain relievers. Her head hurt from lack of sleep. It was four o'clock on Monday afternoon, and she hadn't gone to bed yet because she'd worked all night.

"Oh, for the love of chocolate." Ruth sputtered as she dumped out the contents and rifled through them.

"What's up?" Natalie Stanton, another donation coordinator, stuck her head through Ruth's door. The perky brunette looked like she'd just had an eight-hour nap.

"Headache. Why are you so bright-eyed and bushytailed? We both worked last night, yet you look marvelous while I resemble something the neighbor's cat dragged in."

Natalie shimmied, for lack of a better description, across the drab brown carpet and parked her derriere on the edge of Ruth's desk. "That's because I slept on the flight back. Yours was local. Looking for these?"

Reaching beneath the pile of receipts, her coworker pulled out the hidden bottle and handed it to Ruth. Ruth twisted off the lid, popped two pills into her mouth and then swallowed them with her lukewarm coffee. "Thanks for finding them."

"Can I talk to you a second?" Natalie started to organize the pile of purse contents littering Ruth's desk.

"Sure. What's up?" Surprised, but too tired to chastise her coworker for pawing through her personal stuff, Ruth rubbed her temples to expedite her relief.

"What do you think about that new charter service we've been working with?"

Ruth's stomach lurched, and she couldn't be absolutely certain the painkillers were responsible. Glancing at the hardened expression on Natalie's face, she knew her turmoil had nothing to do with her lack of sleep or her headache. She chose her words carefully. "I think they're competent. More than competent. Why?"

With dread, Ruth anticipated Natalie's rant. The woman's beautiful exterior covered a small, petty and vindictive interior. More than once, Ruth had tried to show her the way of the Lord, but had been met with only resistance.

"Well, I think they should be fired. Brad is nice in a yummy sort of way and the other one never says much, but that Noah character reminds me of Scrooge. He never smiles, and he doesn't treat us very nicely. He was better last night, but still, I don't like him."

And Noah had been doing so well, or at least he had a few days ago. Had something changed since yesterday? Butterflies took flight in her stomach. Regardless of what

Noah thought, or continued to think, Ruth didn't believe that Desert Wings Aviation should be fired. She didn't know much about how contracts were awarded, or how easily they could be broken, but the gleam in her coworker's eyes meant Natalie would stop at nothing to get it done if possible.

Noah must have ticked Natalie off because he didn't respond to her coworker's blatant flirtations. Her conquests with pilots, doctors and other male staff was legendary at the network. The lives of those who didn't succumb to Natalie's wiles were made miserable.

Good for you, Noah.

"He may not be the nicest pilot we've had, but do you have a problem with how he flies the plane?" Ruth was glad her voice didn't show any reaction to the man's name.

Noah had snuck under her radar and caused a chemical reaction best left for the science lab. In fact, if Ruth didn't know better she'd think she'd fallen in love…nonsense. Love didn't factor in to how she felt about the man. Ruth started stuffing the contents her coworker had organized on her desk back into her tan leather purse. Her heartbeat accelerated. The image of Noah beat out the headache behind her right eye.

Natalie sniffed, a sure sign that Ruth had been added to her "them against me" list. The other coordinator tapped the desk with her long manicured fingernails and stared at her. "No. I have no problem with how he flies. Be that as it may, it's his attitude that bothers me. And quite frankly, I don't think his company should have the privilege of making money off of us unless he has a major attitude adjustment. What time do you think Ernie will be in this morning?"

A frown gathered on Ruth's lips at the mention of their boss. Natalie was determined to make Noah's life miserable again just when he'd opened up. His interactions with Tommy and the other children confirmed that. A cold lump wedged its way into Ruth's throat. She needed to protect Noah because God had crossed their paths for a reason. "Please don't say anything to Ernie yet. I'll go talk to Noah, okay? Be a sport and give him another chance."

An hour later, Ruth found herself at the front door of Noah's condo. Her heart raced as if she'd just run the fifty-yard dash. Her gaze slid past the blue paint to the tiny circular light of the doorbell set inside a metal dog paw. She knew in her heart this was what she needed to do. Noah had made progress in the short time she'd known him. She couldn't let Natalie win.

Ruth rang the bell and shifted in her black sandals. Using her hand as a fan, she managed to move the warm, slightly humid air around her and turned to her left to admire the sweeping scenery of the McDowell Mountains, which painted a picture of contentment and beauty. A crested saguaro stood guard next to the wrought iron railing surrounding a tiny stamp of green lawn beyond the neighbor's flagstone patio.

A profusion of fuchsia bougainvilleas and yellow and orange birds of paradise hid the cinder block wall and added to the sense of heaven among the hot, dusty surroundings.

"Nice view, here. Sure beats looking at the neighbor's cinder block wall and ornery cat." Ruth spoke to herself.

From the side of the condo, Houston barked, ran skittering around the corner and then jumped up on her Capri-covered leg. Her lips molded into a smile.

"Hi, Houston. How ya doing?" Ruth leaned over to pat him on the head. "I've missed you, you silly dog. Did you miss me? I'm glad you and Noah got little Tommy to open up. I just wish I could locate a new heart for both him and Marissa—and soon."

Houston barked and licked her hand. A small gust of wind played with the leaves of the olive tree strategically placed to cast the small porch into shade from the afternoon sun. Houston's wet nose felt good against her heated skin before he wriggled around in circles.

"Ruth?" Seconds later, Noah rounded the same corner as his dog with a large manila envelope in his grasp. Dirt and cobwebs covered him from head to toe. He stared at her in surprise and ran a hand through his hair before he brushed the front of his shirt. "Hi. What are you doing here?"

"Hi, Noah. I, um, stopped by to talk to you. It's important." Ruth bit her lip as her gaze wandered down the strong column of his neck to stare at his maroon-colored polo shirt. The spot that covered his heart to be exact.

She could almost see its beat match the rhythm of her own.

"Must be important to bring you to my doorstep. What's up?"

Ruth bowed her head and prayed for strength and guidance. She prayed that Noah would accept what she had to say and be able to move past it.

"Noah, I realize that you still have a problem with flying medical teams around. Knowing about Jeremy, and who you dealt with at the time, I can accept that. You've come a long way since that first flight together, but others from my company can't."

"What's that supposed to mean?" Noah flipped his gaze back to stare at her and drew his eyebrows together.

"It means that one of the coordinators wants to file a complaint with my company about your attitude. She also wants them to terminate the contract. She doesn't feel

Desert Wings Aviation is a good fit." Her voice softened and she breathed in the clean scent of Noah, which brought back instant memories of the companionship she felt with him, a friendship she wanted to deepen into something more permanent. The next thing she knew, she found herself in Noah's open arms, her head against his chest. "I don't want to see that happen. I think our company needs you. I know I do."

"I've really messed things up, haven't I? We need that contract to survive."

Noah gathered her close, and she gloried in the feelings he evoked. Love presided in her rapidly beating heart. "It's nothing we can't fix."

"I'm glad you're here. And that you're on my side." Noah spoke softly as they stood on the tiny front porch outside his condo. Having Ruth in his arms chased away his lingering loneliness and cemented the decision he'd made yesterday. "I'm finally ready to look through the letters from the recipients of Jeremy's organs."

As he rested his chin on top of Ruth's head, his gaze grazed the shadows stretching across his yard, the pale rocks shimmering in the waning sunlight. A rogue bunny hopped under a mesquite tree while a couple of Gambel's quail ran down his driveway. Everything seemed so ordinary, yet what he was about to do was probably the most unordinary thing he'd ever done.

"Yes. I'd be honored to. Thanks for asking me."

"Please, come inside." Noah released Ruth but scooped up her hand before he ushered her into the foyer. Cold air-conditioning blasted them from the vent in the beige-colored wall. He led Ruth down the hallway and into the living room near the back of his condo.

Ruth squeezed his hand, which spoke more than any words she could say. He set the packet down on his coffee table, knowing in his heart it was right for Ruth to be there also. Without her, he wouldn't be ready to face or understand what the letters said. He motioned for her to sit on the love seat, sitting kitty-corner from the sofa. "Would you like something to drink?"

"A glass of water would be great," Ruth responded. Noah noticed her surveying the decidedly masculine room. How well she fit into his life and into his home astounded him. After he opened the letters and put a final closure on Jeremy's death, Noah was determined to explore this attraction between them.

"Make yourself at home. I'll be right back."

Returning from the kitchen, Noah put two glasses of water and a bag of chips on the coffee table before moving the decorative pillow that Houston had knocked over to the other side of the dark brown leather couch.

Then he sat down, ripped open the bag, pulled out a chip and shoved it into his mouth. As he chewed, his gaze transfixed on the manila envelope sitting so innocently on the wood surface. Even though he knew what it contained, he still recoiled.

Confirmation of his guilt.

The letters inside held the information of where the coordinator had scattered Jeremy's organs. Once he read them, it would be impossible to go back. What if his son hadn't really died? What if the doctors could have done more? What if *he* could have done more? What if grief consumed him as thousands of imaginary glass shards shredded his emotions?

Ruth said that it wasn't possible. That brain death was irreversible. That there was nothing else anyone could have done but take what organs still functioned and give them to someone else. Give someone else a chance.

Like Hannah.

Houston whimpered and pawed at Noah's arm. Noah picked up his dog and cradled him close. His fingers wound in the trembling dog's wiry hair as he rubbed his cheek between Houston's ears. The steady beat of Houston's heart grounded him.

Noah had to do this. He was ready. Ruth had revealed more than just his awareness of the good of organ donation. She'd allowed him to feel something else again. Something he'd lost forever. Love.

And something more. Ruth had also awakened his desire to want to know the Lord again and allow Him back into his life.

His gaze took in the woman fingering the rust-colored afghan thrown across the back of the love seat as she sat in his living room like she belonged there. She did.

"That's one of the things my mom knitted. Pretty awful, isn't it?"

Ruth grimaced. "I've seen better, but it's not as bad as that scarf I put on Houston at my place."

Smiling, Noah filled his lungs and stared at the rustic wood coffee table littered with flying magazines. Mistake. He breathed in Ruth's signature scent and toyed with the idea of joining her on the love seat.

He was finally ready. Ready to let go. Ready to open his heart and his mind and to live again.

Noah picked up the manila envelope, unlatched the clasp and dumped the bundle of letters in his lap. As he slipped open the first envelope forwarded to him via the Arizona Organ Donor Network, his fingers trembled.

Letters swam in his vision when he read the letter from

the family of a girl from Tucson a year or so younger than his son's age at the time of his death. She'd received Jeremy's heart. His fingers touched the photograph of the smiling blonde with one of her top teeth missing. Her generous smile touched him.

"Are you okay?" Ruth gripped Noah's hand and squeezed.

Nodding, Noah wiped his face and cleared his throat before he gently pulled his hand from hers. The loss of contact left him bereft and wanting to hold her, but he needed to finish what he started.

"It says here that one of Jeremy's kidneys went to a teenager in Salt Lake City. Take a look." Ruth handed him a photograph of a boy standing by the Great Salt Lake.

Noah opened the third envelope and read the sprawling letters of gratitude that filled the entire page. Another photograph fluttered to the table. "His other kidney and liver went to a woman in California." He paused. "An adult? How is that possible?"

"It depends on the size. As long as the donor organ fits into the recipient, it can go either way. There have been times when an adult organ has gone to a child." Ruth straightened the photo of the black-haired woman. "Believe it or not, Jeremy's organs will continue to grow and become adult sized."

"Amazing." Wonder laced Noah's response.

Noah pulled the picture of his son that he kept in his wallet and set it down amongst the others. Jeremy fit there.

"And his lungs stayed here." Ruth set the final picture down with the others. She laid her head against his shoulder as she wrapped her arm around his waist. Noah didn't pull away because it felt right.

A jigsaw puzzle. Noah traced a line from Jeremy to each recipient. They slipped together, blending, inseparable. One. As if he understood, Houston sniffed at each picture before licking Noah's face.

Noah scratched his dog behind the ears before he sipped his water and wiped his mouth with the back of his hand. He stared at the collage of pictures strewn across his table. People saved because of Jeremy's gift. Beautiful pieces of Jeremy were still alive.

His guilt dissipated when he saw some of the goodness that had come out of Jeremy's death. Another emotion pushed in and made its way to the forefront as he looked at Ruth. Her green eyes shimmered with compassion and understanding and her lightly tinted lips gently curved into the smile that dominated his dreams. Her fragrance surrounded him, pulling him closer to the edge of no return. "Thanks for being here for me today. It means a lot."

He only meant for his mouth to graze the top of her head or the soft skin of her forehead, but when she tilted her head back to look up at him, they found their home on her lips. The whisper of a sigh filled his ears as her eyelids fluttered closed. The brief contact accelerated his heart-beat and left him scared and vulnerable because he wanted more. More than he was able to give her.

Lifting his head, he saw the look of hope residing in her eyes after she opened them. He inched backward on the couch.

"You're welcome. Thanks for inviting me to stay." Ruth recovered quickly, but not before he saw the disappoint-ment flicker across her features.

Disgust filled him. He'd unintentionally hurt her. He changed the subject before he did anything else to ruin the friendship between them. "Is it possible to meet one of these people?" Noah's husky voice still held a trace of emotion. "I want to look into the eyes of one of the recipients who received a piece of Jeremy and thank them for keeping a piece of him alive."

"I don't see why not since they've given you their contact information. The annual donor/recipient picnic is coming up. Why don't you call and see if any of them will be there. If they won't be, we can always drive over and visit them."

Noah hesitated at the way Ruth used the word *we*. As in a couple. As in the two of them. As in together. Love. Their brief kiss affected him on several different levels. Pain forced it to the forefront of his emotions when he thought about what it would be like to lose Ruth like he'd lost Michelle. Maybe he wasn't ready for another relationship. He was falling for her, and it scared him.

He needed to distance himself before it became impossible. He stood and walked over to the picture window, displaying an incredible view of the Sonoran Desert. "Thanks for the offer, but this is something I need to do on my own."

Chapter Twelve

Exhaustion clung to Ruth as she exited the ambulance the following Thursday and dragged her feet across the tarmac to the *Michelle Marie*, the same plane that had dropped her off yesterday. Interesting that Noah had named the plane after his late wife. A sigh hugged her lips.

Today though, instead of Brad's blond head popping out of the doorway, Noah flashed a brief smile as he walked down the steps to meet her. She hadn't seen him since their kiss after he'd opened the letters; yet emotionally, she still felt the connection between them. It sizzled in the air surrounding them and heightened her awareness of him as something more than a friend.

"Hi, Noah." Ruth focused her thoughts on the plane, and she swallowed her anxiety as she toyed with the stress ball inside her pocket. Something didn't feel right.

"Hi, Ruth."

"Where's Houston?" As she glanced at the doorway behind his head, disappointment welled inside her when she realized Noah's dog wasn't inside the plane. Houston had also staked his claim on a piece of her heart, and she could use a little unconditional love right now.

Nothing had gone right in the latter part of the morning for her, and from the uncertain expression on Noah's face, any chance for improvement this afternoon appeared out of the question. He'd pulled away emotionally again.

"He had a long day yesterday, so I left him at home." Noah made no effort to move from the staircase so she could board.

"Oh. Well he deserves a day of rest." The brightness she interjected in her voice fell flat as she stood on the warm tarmac and eyed the sunlight dancing off the white paint of the plane.

A momentary silence hovered in the air as he leaned toward her. His mouth opened and shut quickly before he shifted his attention to the watch around his wrist and tapped the glass surface. "You're done early."

Her fatigue and frustration multiplied. Even though she'd done her best today, she'd still failed. Having a patient code happened to all coordinators. She also viewed it as a test of her faith, which didn't make things easier, and she willed herself not to be so emotional about it in front of Noah.

A tear escaped from beneath her eyelid. Not now. Why couldn't she wait until she was alone to lose her composure? At a loss for words, she shifted on the tarmac, waiting for Noah to move so she could board. Ruth only wanted to sink down in one of the chairs in back and kick off her shoes. Another tear began it's descent.

"Hey. What's wrong." Even his question came out as a statement.

Noah's hand cupped her arm and completed the sense

of companionship lacking in her life. So did his caring expression. More tears slid down her cheeks. Boy, she was tired. Too bad she knew better than to interpret his touch as meaningful, but trying to pry his fingers from her elbow only made her more aware that God never intended His children to carry such a heavy burden alone.

But why Noah? Why now? "You can't help me."

He released her elbow and tilted her chin up with his finger so she had to look in his eyes. The comfort she saw reflected in them frightened her. She'd known better than to get involved with Noah because it would only lead to the heartache and pain she was currently experiencing. Yet she did nothing to stop his thumb from hesitantly touching the trail of tears on her cheeks and smoothing the moisture away. "Try me."

Noah's whisper slipped past the barrier of protection guarding her heart. She closed her eyes and swallowed the grief that had followed her from the hospital. Ruth's fingers curled into fists, bunching the cloth of Noah's shirt, and her rogue tears turned into a torrent of water.

"We lost the donor today. He went into cardiac arrest before we could retrieve any organs." Her voice held another trace of a sob.

"I'm sorry." Noah reached for her hand and gently squeezed, trying to warm her cold fingers. "So that means the people waiting, like Hannah, will have to wait a little longer."

Consumed by the pain, Ruth nodded and leaned her forehead against his chest, feeling his strong, steady heartbeat. A live, beating heart instead of the lifeless one she'd left at the hospital. She hiccupped. "My first one. I feel like I've wasted everyone's time. Mine. The hospital's, the other crews', Brad's, yours." She hiccupped again. "Not only that, I've let down the recipient and his family as well as the donor's family. I don't know why I'm doing this anymore."

The tears multiplied and continued their path down her cheeks. She couldn't stop them even if she wanted to. The release felt good even though Noah's light brown shirt now sported big wet splotches on the front.

"Let it go, Ruth." Noah wrapped his arms around her as a gentle breeze carried sounds of distant traffic closer.

After a commuter plane taxied past, he cradled her to him. Ruth released the front of his shirt and shifted her arms so she could wrap them around Noah's waist. She clung to him and gathered strength from sharing her sorrow with someone who seemed to understand. Someone she'd fallen in love with.

"You do it because there are people out there who need you to do it. People like Hannah and those who received Jeremy's organs. You do it because it's a part of who you are and what you need to do. You're putting this broken world back together one piece at a time." As Noah rubbed her back, she imagined she felt his lips brush the top of her head. He murmured, "It's okay, let it out."

She'd never felt this close to anyone.

Peace settled like a familiar blanket across her shoulders. Her steady stream of tears continued to flow as the rift between them disappeared. Noah understood. Finally.

Ruth fell silent, but Noah could feel her anguish. He wanted to feel it, needed to feel it, because that meant he lived and loved again. Noah tilted her head up and stared into her tear-laden green eyes. The woman in his arms was beautiful. Loving. Caring. Compassionate. All the things he'd been missing.

"You know, this friendship thing isn't working for me."

His lips descended on hers and she responded to his caress. Warm, inviting and alive.

Her fingers inched up to clasp around his neck. She snuggled closer. "Me either. It's all I've thought about."

"You're not the only one." He deepened the kiss. It felt so right to hold her in his arms and kiss her and comfort her. And yet, what he felt had nothing to do with what had happened at the hospital. He fought a losing battle when it came to distancing himself.

Feeling her lips against his was a good thing. Something to be savored. Something he wanted to continue long after the sun set and the darkness of night fell around them. Ruth had made him forget why he shouldn't get involved.

But not completely. What if he lost her, too?

What if he lost the joy that had snuck back into his life when he wasn't looking. The shared tenderness between them lingered as he tasted the coffee and chocolate on her breath and felt her heartbeat match his own. But nothing lasted forever.

With a guttural cry, he pulled his mouth from hers and set a confused and protesting Ruth aside. Sadness devoured his earlier happiness. All good things came to an end. Forcing himself to breathe, he shoved a hand through his hair and stared down at her full, luscious lips made for kissing. He wanted to continue where they'd left off and not worry about the consequences, but harsh reality intruded. He couldn't give Ruth any false hopes that there could ever be anything between them. Because there couldn't be, could there?

Regret laced his words. "I'm sorry, Ruth. That shouldn't have happened. Come on. Let's go."

So why did his lips refuse to forget the promise on hers as he helped her up the stairs?

* * *

Moments after Ruth pulled herself together, took the copilot's seat and wrestled the seat belt over her curves, Noah secured the plane for take-off. Then he folded himself into his own seat and buckled himself in. He handed Ruth a headset before he placed his own over his ears.

With the tiny airport barely a blip on the map, he did a visual before he taxied onto the runway. Ruth had felt so right in his arms. As if she belonged there. As if his holding her had been the most natural thing in the world. As if she was the piece missing out of his life. Maybe he should try? Baby steps, he decided, testing out the idea. A little at a time. Even God had taken six days to create the earth, and on the seventh day He rested. Seven days. Seven minutes. Same thing.

His gaze scraped the eastern sky. Blue. Cloudless. Beckoning. He needed to feel the sense of freedom flying invoked in him, not the emotions Ruth had unleashed inside.

He set the plane in motion. The thrum of rubber cruising over cement vibrated the yoke in his grasp. The bumpy runway smoothed out as he pointed the nose of the King Air 300 into the sky. Beside him, he noticed Ruth clutch her stress ball as a prayer settled on her lips.

"The flight will be okay, Ruth. Relax." He acknowledged her fright.

"Easier said than done." She bit her bottom lip.

With clarity, or stupidity or a bit of both, Noah realized Ruth needed to acknowledge her fears, too. He had confronted what frightened him the other day head-on by learning about the process of organ donation and reading through those recipient letters instead of hiding behind an impregnable wall of silence. He'd also done something else. "I went and talked to Hannah's doctor yesterday."

"Oh? How did it work out?"

"I'm not an eligible candidate." Disappointment settled in his heart again. He'd hoped and had almost got down on his knees to pray that he could supply the kidney his office manager needed. He hadn't even made it past the first interview.

"I'm so sorry. You'll have to give me his name so I can talk to him."

"I'd appreciate that. I know Hannah would, too. So, now that I've faced my fears, are you ready to face yours?" Noah managed to say out loud.

"What makes you think I'm afraid?" Ruth's words tumbled together. Her green eyes widened over her bloodless cheeks. She practically chewed her bottom lip.

A light gust of wind buffeted the plane, and he heard Ruth cry out at the sudden loss of altitude. He slanted a smile in her direction. "Enough said."

Silence lingered inside the plane like an unwelcome air pocket until the plane leveled off.

"Okay, Ruth. We're at cruising altitude. Time for you to fly the plane." Noah's words forced the air from Ruth's lungs.

"Excuse me?" She swallowed, but her saliva refused to budge past the huge lump in her throat. Her teeth buried themselves in her bottom lip, and her stomach contents tumbled around like wet clothes in a dryer.

"I want you to fly the plane."

He released her hand and flipped a switch on the console. Her stomach hit the nonexistent turbulence. "You're nuts. What are you doing?"

"Turning off the autopilot. Now grab the yoke and take control." Noah's voice held no trace of humor.

The man was serious. Utterly serious. Just being inside

of this metal contraption made her uneasy. Flying it would create her nightmare of burning and crashing to the ground a reality.

"But I don't know what I'm doing." When Noah folded his arms over his chest, Ruth bit back her scream. On impulse, she wrapped her fingers around the U-shaped contraption in front of her and continued to chew her lip.

Outside of the initial awkwardness, the yoke didn't feel much different than the steering wheel of a car. Now if she could just forget about all the knobs and gauges staring back at her from the console.

Noah smiled at her. "Relax. It's as easy as riding a bike. You do know how to ride one, don't you?"

Ruth nodded and squirmed in her seat. She knew she should have sat in the back today. In her mind's eye she could visualize the tan leather seat calling to her. "Why are you doing this?"

"Because you'll lose some of your fear of flying if you control the plane for a bit."

"You're asking the impossible." Ruth's white knuckles gleamed as she strangled the yoke. "I don't have a clue how to fly a plane. It takes hours of instruction and flight time. What if we crash? What if a bird flies into the engines? What if a bolt of lightning strikes us?"

"We're not going to crash. A bird isn't going to fly into the engine. And there's not a cloud in the sky right now."

Noah coughed, probably trying to cover his laughter. Ruth thought darkly. "Well, what if you black out and leave me alone to fly the plane?"

This time a soft chuckle sounded in her ears. "Then I guess you'd better know how to fly this thing."

A silent prayer, more like a plea, hissed out on her expended breath. "Good point."

"Now the yoke controls your pitch and roll. Like riding a bike, remember? Try it."

Ruth barely turned the yoke to the left. The aircraft responded and veered slowly off course. Her heartbeat accelerated as she swallowed.

"That's it, Ruth. You're doing great." Noah's soft words of encouragement eased her anxiety. No sarcasm, no snide comments.

She could do this. Her gasp for breath didn't quite seem as urgent now.

"No big movements. Just let the airplane guide you. Now turn slightly back to the right."

Ruth eased the yoke back to the right. Her palms itched. A new sense of exhilaration took hold. She *could* do it. She was flying the plane. Noah trusted her enough to take the controls. Ruth grinned, a smile replacing her earlier frown. A heady sense of excitement and control chased away her anxiety. For the first time in her life, Ruth felt like she had finally started living.

"Now if you want to ascend, pull the yoke back toward you. Push it forward to lower the nose. Easy as that."

Her confidence building, Ruth did as Noah instructed. She found herself enjoying the experience. So far none of the things she'd worried about had transpired. No birds, bolts of lightning or any other hazard had caused the plane to tumble from the sky. For once, she was in control of her destiny thanks to the pilot seated next to her. Well, as in control as God allowed her to be. Laughter bubbled inside and trickled past her lips.

"You're still doing great, Ruth. You're a fast learner. Do you want to roll the plane?" Noah's question evaporated her elation.

Her laughter died. "I don't think so. Flying is one thing.

Turning this baby upside down so that nothing but a thin piece of metal is all that stands between my head and the ground is another."

The moment she turned and looked at his expression she realized he hadn't been serious. What a relief. Until another daunting idea surfaced and caused her stomach to do a somersault instead. "Please tell me you're not going to make me land this thing."

"No. I'll save that for the next lesson." Noah flipped the autopilot back on and reached for his controls. He pushed down to ready for landing, and the plane started to descend. Too bad her stomach decided to stay at the original altitude. Her fingers flew to her midsection in an attempt to bring her innards back in line.

"You really did a great job. Let me know when you want to try again."

Ruth nodded. Noah had taken her fears seriously and helped her face them straight on. She didn't know many men who would do that, much less someone who didn't have some sort of agenda. "I will. Thanks."

Settling back in her seat, she savored the feeling of conquering her fears as the plane continued its descent. From what she could tell from all the dials and screens was that they were at about eight thousand feet and dropping quickly. Her gaze transfixed on the radar, but with a giddy sense of happiness, she realized she had no idea what it represented.

"What does that do?" She pointed to the screen just to the left of Noah.

"That shows rain. As you can see, it's another beautiful day in Scottsdale."

"Gotta love it." As Noah prepared to land, Ruth closed her eyes. Flying wasn't so bad. The heady sense of accomplishment lulled her into a semi-comatose state as another smile drifted to her lips. The man she loved was something else.

At five thousand feet and ten miles out from the Scottsdale Airport, Noah caught a flash of sunlight bouncing off glass and white metal against the blue sky outside the cockpit window. He twisted his neck to the left. His stomach lurched and he inhaled sharply. A high performance sailplane. In the same air space and on a collision course. "Hang on."

Seconds too late, he yanked back on the yoke. The tip of the King Air rose a fraction before the impact. A loud thud shocked his ears, and an intense shudder ripped through the plane. Noah's guttural cry was sucked out of the cockpit through the gaping hole to the left of his seat.

"What happened?" The tightness in Ruth's voice intensified his apprehension. Muscles bunched in his neck and shoulders as he fought to keep them airborne and from rolling over.

"A sailplane just hit us." Turbulence rattled the plane and the teeth inside his mouth. All the training and simulations didn't prepare him for the reality of a real in-flight emergency. The hole beside his left leg mocked his attempt to remain calm and focused.

"How did that happen? Why didn't you see it with the radar or something?" Ruth's terrified whisper grabbed his heart and yanked it outside his chest. Her hands clenched in a death grip.

"I saw it at the last minute and my avoidance system only shows planes with transponders. Sailplanes don't typically have them. Getting a visual on it any earlier than I did would have been like finding a needle in a haystack."

His voice seeped out like a leaking balloon. He radioed a distress call and forced himself to stay calm. He couldn't focus on the other pilot; he had enough to worry about. Like keeping the woman he loved safe.

His grip tightened on the yoke. He'd lost all his electronics. The only thing he could do now was manually keep the nose up, head the plane in the direction of the Scottsdale Airport and say a prayer.

Except he still didn't pray. He figured now probably wasn't the time to start. No. Praying was left to those who completely believed and obeyed God's word. They didn't question His motives or actions, or turn away from Him.

"You'd better start praying, Ruth. One of us needs to, and I can't do it." Noah's voice seeped though clenched teeth and enunciated each syllable.

A shattered gasp erupted from the other side of the cockpit. Noah didn't pull his gaze from the scene beyond the window. He had a visual on the airport now, the office buildings and businesses surrounding it and the commuter traffic snaking along Frank Lloyd Wright Boulevard. If he didn't make it to the airport in less than two minutes, they'd be dead.

Tension tore at Noah's nerves and bile scraped the back of his throat. He had no room to turn around, no room to make a judgment in error. Nowhere to go.

He dared to glance at Ruth, hoping it wouldn't be the last time. Her bloodless face and trembling lips ripped at his fragile emotions. He would keep her safe, even if it killed him.

"Why won't you pray with me?" she whispered. "There's power in numbers."

"I can't." He looked out the front window again. A band of sweat broke out on his forehead and underneath his arms. But was it because of the imminent emergency landing, or the words Ruth wanted him to say? He might be a lot of things, but he wasn't a hypocrite. Why would God listen to him anyway? He hadn't before when Noah had cried out to Him to save Jeremy's life.

Yet maybe. Just maybe… "I don't know what to say."

The plane lost more altitude. A band of sweat gathered on his brow, and he struggled to keep the plane upright.

"It's like riding a bike. You remember how to do that, don't you?"

A heaviness permeated the cabin as the airport loomed in front of them. Funny time for Ruth to twist his words around.

"Yes. But I may be a little rusty." He hadn't ridden a bike or said a prayer since he'd left Michelle's and Jeremy's bodies at the hospital.

"Then just say what's in your heart."

Right. As if it was that easy.

"I don't think the Lord wants to hear my fear. Just say something. Anything," Noah ground out. The plane was losing speed now, and he doubted they'd make the runway. He heard the engines sputter.

An old proverb surfaced in his mind: The Lord will hear when I call to Him.

Could Noah take the chance? Would God listen this time?

His mouth opened but nothing tumbled out.

Fortunately, Ruth had enough panicked words for both of them. "Dear God. Help us land safely. Keep us in Your loving hands. Especially Noah. Your will be done. Amen."

"Amen." The word slipped out and temporarily calmed him.

The plane slowed even more and began to vibrate. They

dropped more altitude. The McDowell Mountains loomed like a sleeping dragon to his left. The Scottsdale Princess Resort, golf course and housing community were a distant memory behind them. The light gray strip of runway hovered like a beacon on a dark night.

"Why aren't you putting down the landing gear?" Ruth's strangled cry cast goose bumps across his skin.

"Too risky. It'll create a drag. We're unstable enough as it is." He strangled the shuddering yoke as if he could keep the plane up by sheer will. In a few seconds he'd know if he was successful or not.

Noah eased up to level the plane. They'd cleared the buildings. They had barely enough altitude to avoid the street. The engine sputtered again, and he almost took out the light pole. Then nothing but a fence and runway now.

Perspiration stung his eyes, but they cleared the fence. The clear, wide expanse of concrete spread out before him.

"Brace yourself. Three, two, one."

With a loud, hard thud, the belly of the plane connected with ground. The impact jarred every cell in his body.

Metal chafed the cement.

The yoke vibrated violently beneath his palms, while Ruth's terrified screams filled his ears. His own sounds joined with hers and competed with the interior noise of plane as it careened down the runway.

Without landing gear in place, Noah had no brakes.

He had no steering.

He had no control.

The King Air shuddered and scraped along the strip of cement, the noise almost tearing his eardrums apart. Seconds stretched into eternity, yet collapsed in upon themselves.

Fence. Buildings. Other planes whirled by the window in a kaleidoscope of objects.

Then the plane slid sideways. More adrenaline raced in his veins as he fought to control the spin. Useless. Nausea won the battle in his stomach. His shoulder slammed into the side of the plane, and pain radiated through his being.

Dirt and dust blinded the outside view as the aircraft's momentum continued to spin in circles. Clutching his bad arm, Noah bowed his head and braced himself for a collision.

After a seemingly nonending, teeth shattering, mind-numbing moment, the plane shuddered to a halt. The chink of metal reverberated through the interior. He stared at the brown dirt through the hole by his foot and expelled his breath before lifting his gaze to look through the broken window. The plane had tangled in the chain link fence at the end of the runway. Dead silence hovered inside the cockpit.

They'd survived the landing, but they weren't safe yet.

"Ruth?"

No answer. Fear clutched him in its grip again. Smoke and dust burned his eyes. His gaze slid past Ruth as he swiveled around and saw flames licking at the rear of the plane. His heartbeat accelerated but not because of the fire.

"Ruth."

Unconsciousness had claimed her and blood trickled down her cheek from the gash in her forehead. A piece of the metal railing speared through the cockpit and rested against her chest. Anger curled in his gut. He hadn't kept her safe as he'd promised.

Chapter Thirteen

Why, Lord. Why?

No answer, but what had he really expected? Still, he found himself reaching out. *Please Lord, let Ruth be okay. I love her.*

More adrenaline kicked in. With determined fingers, Noah unbuckled his seat belt, yanked off his headset and threw it to the ground. Then he unbuckled Ruth. A cough filled his throat and smoke burned his eyes as he gingerly pulled off her headset and threw it in the same direction as he'd done with his. The smell of jet fuel filled his lungs. "Come on, baby. We've got to get out of here."

Using brute strength, he forced the twisted metal away from her. Then he set his fingers against the pulse point on her neck and felt a shallow beat. At least she was alive. For now. Ignoring the pain radiating down his arm, he slid it behind her shoulders and his other good arm under her knees and lifted. Then he felt his way to the door, forced it open and carried Ruth down the stairs.

"Thank you, Lord," Noah whispered.

God did exist.

He'd felt something right after Ruth's prayer. A presence that seemed to guide the plane, cradle it, making sure it made the runway and came to a stop without crumbling into pieces. Noah couldn't quite explain what had happened.

It wasn't that easy, couldn't be that easy.

Rogue tears fell from his eyes and traveled down his cheeks.

Men didn't cry. At least not in public.

But then again, most men hadn't just walked away from a plane crash.

Heat seared his exposed skin and dried the moisture. Noah welcomed the solid ground beneath his feet as he held on to Ruth and moved them farther away from the aircraft.

Sirens screamed in his ears as a fire truck and ambulance screeched to a halt on the tarmac close to where the plane rested. Firemen and paramedics ran toward them.

"Anyone else inside?" A voice questioned.

Noah shook his head and gently placed Ruth on the ground so the paramedics could look her over. He backed away, adrift from the loss of contact, yet he knew the two men needed room to work. Another paramedic wearing a blue T-shirt approached. "Let's take a look at you."

"I'm fine." Noah waved him off. The next few minutes playing out in front of him as if he were a phantom spectator. Firemen and policemen scurried about like frenzied ants. Paramedics brought out a stretcher and loaded a still-unconscious Ruth on it. Above him, helicopters captured the scene to replay over and over again for the evening news. Finally, his feet carried him forward to Ruth's side, her face almost as pale as the white sheet underneath her. He picked up her hand and held it close to his heart. Then he leaned over and brushed her forehead with his lips. "I love you. Please don't die on me. Please."

A hand clasped his shoulder. "I'm sure she'll be fine. You coming along for the ride?"

Noah straightened and shook his head. He had to stay here and deal with the plane and the men in suits heading his way. A soft moan escaped from Ruth's lips, and he thought he felt her squeeze his hand before he set it down. Then he watched helplessly as a paramedic took Ruth to the ambulance, loaded her in and disappeared, taking her out of his life.

He watched the firemen put out the flames consuming the entire rear section of his favorite plane. A total loss. *Michelle Marie* was truly gone from his life now and he didn't just mean the airplane. Closure washed over him. Michelle was dead, but Ruth wasn't. Not if he could help it.

He continued to stare at the damage to the front part of the plane he could see. The entire nose of the aircraft was gone. Wires protruded from where the metal had ripped away. The wing was damaged, and part of the propeller didn't exist anymore. A piece of metal from the sailplane stuck out from the body of the plane where the hole inside had been. They were lucky to be alive.

Noah finally found the courage and strength to bow his head and pray that the other pilot had survived and for Ruth's recovery.

Grueling hours later, after Noah had filled out mounds of paperwork, he found himself sitting in his truck in the deserted airport parking lot, staring blankly at the windshield. Darkness scraped the outside of the glass and his anxiety built in waves, ready to tear down the lone remaining wall surrounding his heart. He gasped for breath.

The scent of smoke permeating from Ruth's overnight bag and computer lying in the passenger seat assaulted his nostrils and unraveled the thin thread holding his emotions together. He'd retrieved them once he'd been let inside his damaged aircraft. He'd also taken the small photo frame with Michelle and Jeremy's picture in it from the side compartment. Nothing else inside the plane had any value.

His life would have no meaning again if anything had happened to Ruth.

With Houston in Brad's care for the time being, Noah turned the key and started the engine. He stopped his fingers from shaking by gripping the steering wheel. He had to find Ruth. He had to see her to apologize and make sure she was okay. If she'd even regained consciousness.

Having no idea where they'd taken her, he thrust a hand through his hair before throwing the truck in reverse and backing out of the space. Then he shoved the vehicle into drive and made his way toward the entrance. There were only so many hospitals in the Scottsdale area. He'd find her.

"May I help you?" The matronly looking E.R. nurse with dark circles under her eyes barely glanced in Noah's direction as she stared at the computer screen.

Noah rubbed the back of his hand across the coarse stubble on his chin. He glanced around the sparsely populated emergency room, hoping for the unlikely chance that he'd spot Ruth. Only the white walls, a Hispanic family with a sick-looking child and an elderly gentleman in a wheelchair graced the interior. He turned his attention back to the nurse. "I'm looking for Ruth Fontaine? She would have been brought in about four o'clock this afternoon?"

"Hmm. That name sounds familiar." After the woman

tapped some letters on her keyboard, her brows furrowed "Yes, she's here. Are you family?"

"Family? No." Noah's stomach clenched. Something was wrong. Had Ruth been hurt more than he or the paramedics suspected?

"I'm sorry, sir. Unless you're family, visiting hours are over." At least the woman looked contrite as she looked back down at the computer screen in front of her. "Why don't you try back tomorrow?"

More nausea unsettled the coffee in his stomach. He balled his fists on the counter and inhaled sharply. The oxygen did little to calm his tense nerves. "Can you at least tell me if she's okay? Please?"

"I'm afraid I can't. All I can tell you is visitors are allowed in at seven o'clock. Excuse me." The nurse reached to pick up the ringing phone next to her left hand

"Fine. I'll wait." He gave the woman a curt nod and spun on his heel. Then he strode toward the most comfortable looking chair in the waiting room and settled his weary body into the burgundy material and prepared for a long wait. He wasn't leaving until he saw Ruth.

In the stillness of the late evening, Ruth found the strength to open her eyes again. Sleep continued to elude her. Staring at the while hospital walls draped in shadows was better than replaying the whole crash scene that flashed behind her eyelids. Fear rode in on her panicked breath. She could still hear the horrific noise and feel the intense heat from the flames. Her hands clutched at the white sheets beneath her, entangling the fabric in her fingers until she also remembered the comforting feel of Noah's arms around her when he carried her from the wreckage.

Ruth wanted to feel that safety and security again. She also wanted to hear the words Noah whispered to her in the chaos before the blackness claimed her. Did he really say he loved her? Or was it a figment of her imagination? Or had he said those words because he thought they were what she wanted to hear?

Ruth shifted, but she couldn't escape her thoughts. Her entire body continued to ache and her head throbbed where she'd hit it, but she was alive thanks to Noah. Where was he? Had he been hurt in the crash, too?

Ruth struggled with the thin sheet covering her body. She had to find out. Stars danced in her vision when she tried to sit up, but due to her lack of strength, the top sheet only bunched itself tighter around her legs. Dismayed and disgusted, she fell back on the pillow as a figure appeared in the doorway. Her heart raced. Noah?

"Hey, there, Ruth. How you feeling?" Samantha had popped in. "I was so worried about you."

"I've had better days." Disappointment pooled in her stomach and slumped her shoulders. Ruth forced a smile to her best friend. Even that seemed to hurt. "How'd you hear?"

Samantha pulled up a chair next to the bed and sat down. "Mark called me. He heard it on the scanner. I would have come earlier but I just got off work."

"That's okay. I'm glad your husband wasn't one of the paramedics. It probably would have freaked him out."

"Nah. He's a professional." Concern laced Samantha's voice as she reached over and picked up Ruth's hand. The gentle contact soothed her. "So, what's wrong? Why are you still here?"

"As a precaution. I took a pretty nasty blow to the head."

"So that explains the bandage. Good. Now maybe you'll get some much needed rest."

"Right. Like that's going to happen with the nurses checking on me all the time. You of all people ought to know better." A tiny snort spilled through Ruth's lips.

Samantha squeezed her fingers and hovered close to the bed like a mother hen. "Look. When they release you, I want you to stay with us for a few days, okay? I'll get my shifts covered, and it will be like old times when we roomed together in nursing school."

Ruth would probably get more rest if she went home, but she didn't want to disappoint her friend. "That sounds awesome. Thanks for the offer." Her gaze slid from Samantha's face to the blank television screen and then back. Ruth had to know. She couldn't really rest until she found out. "Can you do me a favor?"

"Sure. What do you need?"

"I need to know that Noah's okay. He was the pilot." Uncertainty arose, and Ruth's eyes filled with tears.

Samantha's expression softened. "You love him, don't you?"

Ruth nodded.

"Let me go check for you. I'll be right back." Samantha rushed from the room.

Five minutes later, she returned, a small frown creasing her forehead. "He's not here. You came in alone. Noah refused treatment at the scene, but Mark talked to one of the paramedics who said the pilot didn't appear to have any injuries, so I'm guessing he's okay. Look, I gotta run now. I want to stop by your house and grab some clean clothes for you. Call me when they release you, and one of us will come pick you up."

"Thanks, Samantha. I will."

Once her friend left, Ruth closed her heavy, sleep-laden eyelids. *Where are you, Noah? I need you.*

* * *

Noah's footsteps dragged along the long corridor at eight o'clock the next morning. His entire body hurt, probably a residual effect from the accident and the long, uncomfortable stay in the waiting room chair downstairs. Somehow he'd managed to sleep, but no matter which way he turned, comfort eluded him. Was the discomfort more from the furniture or his mind's inability to shut off the kaleidoscope of images that hunted him? The crash. The fire. An unconscious Ruth.

And the realization that he loved her.

Had she woken up yet? If the hospital staff downstairs knew, no one would tell him.

His feet rooted to the linoleum floor. What if she hadn't make it? What if— Gasping for breath he leaned against the cold, unforgiving wall and closed his eyes. He didn't know what scared him the most. His feelings for her or the idea that her injury was fatal. Or maybe it was both.

Nonsense. Ruth was okay. They wouldn't let him see her if something bad had happened.

Dread crept in and attacked any progress he'd made. Images of that other hospital hall from three years earlier filled his brain. Could he handle this again? Nerves frayed, he almost punched a hole in the foam cup of coffee he carried.

Outside of room twenty-one, Noah froze. Ruth was inside. Could his heart take seeing her lying in a hospital bed? Could his brain allow him to walk away from her?

The uncertainty of the last twelve hours had only confirmed his decision. It had to be this way. He had to let her go. It was in her best interest. He couldn't face the possibility of hurting her again. So why did he feel so rotten?

Gasping for air, he filled his lungs with the disinfectant-laden hospital air and trudged through the wide doorway. His gaze immediately went to the opposite side, to where the pristine bed waited to swallow the next patient. His attention lurched to the closest bed, where a motionless Ruth lay in a half-sitting position. With her eyes closed and the riot of blond curls haloing her pale face, she reminded him of a sleeping angel. Only a bandage on her forehead and the hospital gown signaled her close brush with death.

Nausea hit him full force.

"Ruth?" His whisper barely registered over the sound from the television, yet her eyelids fluttered open.

"Hi, Noah. I'm so glad you're okay."

Her smile lit up the room, and his darkness receded. Momentarily. Guilt reached out its sharp, merciless claws and grappled him again. "How are you feeling? How bad are you hurt?"

"I got nothing more than a few cuts and bruises and I'm sore, but I'll heal. Keeping me overnight was simply a precaution. I'm waiting for the doctor to release me." Her voice softened and sounded like melted butter on a homemade biscuit, which made him want to forget why he'd come and try to figure out how to start over. "Thanks to you, it wasn't worse."

"Here. I brought you a few things." Uncomfortable at her seemingly herolike worship of him, Noah set the big vase of flowers on the tray table next to the water jug. Then he held out the cup in her direction before he put her overnight bag and laptop on the floor near the bed. "I know how lousy hospital coffee is so I walked down the street to the coffee shop. I made it just the way you like it."

"Two creamers and one sweetener?" Her fingers touched his as she took the proffered cup. The inexplicable feeling that they belonged together clouded his thinking.

He reeled from the contact and moved away from the bed. "Yes."

"Thanks, Noah. The flowers are beautiful, too. How did you know I prefer a mixed bouquet?"

"I saw the silk flowers on the shelf in your living room." Noah shifted uncomfortably, yet his traitorous eyes continued to stare at Ruth. Somehow he'd never be able to look at another flower arrangement or a pink sweetener without thinking of how the woman in front of him had changed his life for the better.

"Oh. Would you like a seat?" Ruth motioned to the chair at the head of the bed.

"No, thanks. I won't be here that long."

Ruth's smile dipped as she took a sip of her coffee. As she continued to stare at him over the lip of the cup, her eyes widened in confusion. "Why did you walk to the coffee shop, Noah? Why are you still in the same clothes? Are you hurt? Did you spend the night here, too? Samantha said you weren't admitted."

She filled the sudden silence while her fingers bunched the top sheet. "Of course. There's got to be tons of paperwork to fill out. The plane's a complete loss, isn't it?"

Noah nodded. But the plane was the least of his worries. He had insurance. Getting through the rest of his life without Ruth was the real heartbreaking thought. He had to get out of here before he did something stupid—like confess his love.

"I'm so sorry. I know you loved that plane. But the important thing is that we all survived. I heard on the early news that the glider pilot is okay. He parachuted to safety after impact." Ruth stretched out her arm but let it drop to her side.

Noah shifted his weight. "I'd also heard that."

He wanted to lean forward and kiss her again. He wanted to feel the softness of her lips against his as he'd felt on the tarmac at Rio Salado City. Except if he kissed her again his resolve would waver. He couldn't risk it.

"Is there something bothering you?" Ruth's fingers tightened around the cup. Coffee sloshed though the tiny hole and spilled onto her hand.

Looking for a way to keep busy, Noah grabbed a tissue from the box on the tray and dabbed her fingers, the scent of coffee overriding the lingering odor of disinfectant. His voice wobbled under the strain of his words. "I'm sorry, Ruth. I came to apologize."

As her hand stilled on his, he lost himself in the depths of her eyes. He wanted to memorize every detail of her. Today her irises were a murky moss-green and filled with confusion.

"Apologize for what?"

"For the accident. I promised to keep you safe, and I failed." His voice cracked.

Groaning slightly, Ruth pushed herself up in the hospital bed and stared up at him, her eyebrows pulled together in a frown. "How can you say that? The accident was just that. An accident. You had no control over what the other pilot did or didn't do."

Noah shoved a hand through his hair and stepped back from the bed. He couldn't stop the accident scene from replaying in a continuous loop inside his head. "That doesn't matter. I take full responsibility. I should have seen it coming."

"This is ridiculous, Noah, and you know it. Next thing you'll be telling me is that our friendship is off." Ruth closed her eyes, placed her fingers to her forehead and then began to rub.

Stricken, Noah could only nod. It had to be this way. He couldn't take the added responsibility of loving Ruth and losing her. Pain radiated from his heart. "It has to be this way. Don't you understand?"

"No, I don't. I care bout you, Noah Barton." She pulled the covers off and gingerly moved her legs to the side of the bed. Noah stood, frozen to the square piece of linoleum as Ruth wrapped the hospital blanket around her shoulders and walked toward him.

She anchored her arms around his waist and rested her head against his chest. He reciprocated. Holding her was right, but that was where it had to end. Savoring the moment to remember for later, he rested his chin against the crown of her head. Their hearts beat together, united. Untwining her arms, he picked her up and gently carried her back to the hospital bed and set her down on the white sheets. He pulled the covers over her, his fingers grazing the softness of her cheek.

Tears filled her eyes as she stared up at him. He was shutting her out. "Don't do this, Noah. Don't you at least care about me a little?"

Refusing to answer, he turned and stumbled from the room.

The scent of vanilla wafted from the lit candle next to Ruth's computer monitor while the light sound of jazz played from the built-in speaker. The stillness of her house at eight o'clock on a Tuesday evening settled around her in a comfortable familiarity. Cradling her head between her hands, she stifled a yawn. Four days had passed since the accident, three days since she'd been released from the hospital, and yet she still ached.

Now she understood why people said they'd felt like

they'd been hit by a semitruck. She knew firsthand and groaned as she stretched her arms over her head. Maybe she should have spent another night at her friend's house. At least Samantha's four-year-old daughter, Kylie, had kept Ruth entertained.

Ruth needed to get back to work. The inactivity grated on her type A personality. It would also keep her mind occupied so she could forget about Noah.

Grief clung to her and refused to release her from its grasp. She'd chosen wrong again. Beyond tired, she wondered if her job or even remaining in Arizona was really all worth it. Worth the sleepless nights, the odd hours and the aggravation of too few organs for everyone that needed them. So far, no heart had become available for Marissa, and time was running out. The little girl had taken another turn for the worse, and there was nothing short of a miracle that could change it.

Ruth stared at the bulletin board on the opposite wall where she'd hoped to place Marissa's picture some day. A collage of pictures of survivors stared back at her. The smiling Tabitha, with blond hair and chubby cheeks. Nathaniel, the Asian boy standing on a dock next to what looked like his brother. And then there was Claudia, the baby with the big blue eyes in a pink onesie that read "Mommy's little blessing."

A gift from heaven. A tear trickled down Ruth's cheek.

Each one of these children had one thing in common.

Each one carried a donor organ.

An organ she'd help place.

Ruth's hand touched the butterfly bracelet around her wrist. Her near brush with death last week had made her more aware of how precious life was and how it could abruptly change.

Ruth stared at a photo of her and Rachel on her antique desk. Even though they were identical twins, most people had no problem telling them apart. Rachel had always been the paler, skinnier twin, more fragile because of her disease.

Ruth's fingers grazed the surface of the frame as if trying to reach back in time to touch her sister again. Rachel's curly blond hair had blown in the slight breeze as they'd puttered around in their tiny rowboat on Bragg's Lake near the Wisconsin Dells. The sun shone brightly, sparkling off the tiny waves. The lapping water against their boat had been rhythmic and soothing.

This Indian summer day in early September had been their last day on the lake together. Rachel had grown too weak to go out in the boat, and by the next summer, she was gone.

Sometimes just looking at her sister's picture was more than Ruth could bear. A steady stream of tears coursed down her cheeks. The box of tissues by the phone remained untouched. It was almost as if Ruth needed to purge herself instead of hiding everything behind a wall of efficiency.

When her sister died, the fragile string that connected them together unraveled. She hadn't felt complete until she'd fallen in love with Noah. Judging by his lack of communication since she'd left the hospital, he hadn't changed his mind.

Noah's image dallied in her consciousness. She ached at the haunted shadows beneath his eyes. She cried even harder at the image of the way the crow's feet deepened when he dared to laugh. His tender kiss after she'd lost her first donor had made her feel loved and cherished.

She loved a man who couldn't let himself love her in return.

Her gaze strayed back to the picture in the gray metallic frame embedded with rhinestones. She couldn't help Rachel now, but she helped other children and adults. She helped spare other parents and siblings the anguish and despair over losing a loved one.

A viselike grip tightened over her heart. Was Ruth reliving the past? Was she so focused on what had happened that, like Noah, she'd had difficulties putting it all behind her? Was that what the pictures scattered across her wall were all about?

Dropping her head to rest on the scarred surface, Ruth sighed in frustration as her fingers curled into balls. She banged them on the desk, upsetting her desk organizer. Several paper clips jumped out and scattered across the top, the noise upsetting the stillness of the night. Her monitor woke from its screen saver, the blinking cursor inside the search box signaling for her to input information.

What information?

That Ruth was a fraud? That her undying need to help others was really just a way for her to stay in the past instead of dealing with her real issues like letting her sister's memory rest? Because Noah wasn't the only one with past issues, pretending to go through daily living.

Maybe she shouldn't have been so set against going to therapy when her parents had suggested it. Maybe she could have worked through her issues instead of pushing them away. More tears followed the path made by the ones before.

Did she still have it in her to be an organ donation coordinator? If Marissa didn't make it, she didn't know if she could stand it anymore. Was this what burnout felt like? She'd heard it happened, but usually around the three-year mark.

Forcing herself from the office, she retreated to the kitchen to grab a pint of chocolate ice cream from the freezer. Her bare feet slapped against the tile floor all the way to her couch. Gingerly, she lowered herself onto the soft surface and sank down onto the cushions. Sorting through the mail that had somehow manifested into a pile on her coffee table, she spied the annual invitation to the donor/recipient family picnic sponsored by Arizona Organ Donor Network scheduled for this coming weekend.

Her hands trembled as she slid open the flap and took the slip of paper out. As she read over the words, her earlier frustrations disappeared. She still had more coordinations in her.

Okay, Lord. I get it. You're not going to let me give up, are you?

Saturday afternoon at the large park in central Phoenix, Noah wiped his damp palms across his jeans as he leaned against a palm tree. It wasn't the heat from the sun shining through the fronds that made him hot and uncomfortable. The day had dawned mild, a sure sign the summer furnace-like temperatures stretched out behind them like an endless dream. Nor did the park filled with strangers cause his hands to shake. No. Only the ten-year-old girl that had agreed to meet him at the donor/recipient family picnic could have that affect on him.

He felt the urge to run until his legs burned and his lungs hurt with exertion. And keep going until he couldn't run anymore from the people, the park and the evidence that God did work miracles on Earth through people like Ruth. But he couldn't run from his memories, or his emotions or his faith anymore.

He bowed his head and prayed. *Lord, give me strength.*

*You've brought me this far. Please be with me when I meet
Jessica.*

He tested and tasted the words again. It was like riding
a bike. He'd wobbled at first, rusty from disuse, and at
times like now, he could use some training wheels. Or
Ruth. But he'd made his decision in the hospital not to see
her anymore and had even pulled himself off rotation for
any calls from AeroFlight. He'd almost killed her. His
heart just wasn't strong enough to continue to love her and
lose her like he'd almost done.

Staying against the tree, he stared at the pigeon strut-
ting around the garbage can off to his left. Occasionally,
the gray bird would find something interesting to peck at,
and more pigeons fluttered to the ground. The biggest one
stared up at Noah with a beady eye as his head dipped up
and down, searching for an elusive crumb left behind by
some picnic goer. A quick glance at his watch told him that
in a few minutes his life would be altered again—but in a
more positive way.

He glanced at his watch again. Doubt filled him, and
he wished Ruth would be by his side when he met Jessica
for the first time. Maybe he shouldn't have been so hasty
in his decision.

He missed Ruth. And with a blinding certainty, he
realized that he needed her in his life. Going through life
alone was far worse than taking another chance on love.
And he knew without a doubt that he loved her.

And that he'd messed up.

But then again, with God, everything was possible. Or he
prayed it was where Ruth was concerned. Spying a familiar,
tall brunette, Noah suddenly had the chance to fix something
else, too. He intercepted the woman as she walked past.
"Excuse me, Natalie. May I talk to you a second?"

Natalie's stare made him uncomfortable because he knew she was the coordinator who complained about him. But was it because of his old attitude or the fact he'd sloughed off her advances? Her gaze roved over him and she smiled. "Sure."

Ignoring the signal she sent out, he shoved a hand through his hair. "Look, Natalie. I'm sorry if I offended you in any way. I've had some issues to work out both professionally and personally. You're a beautiful woman, but I'm not really your type. My heart is spoken for. I—I'm in love with Ruth."

It felt good to get that off his chest, but he hadn't told the right woman.

Natalie's expression softened and she sighed. "Apology accepted. I wasn't really going to try to get your contract terminated, you know. My bark is worse than my bite. Good luck to you and Ruth. See you on the next fly out."

With a toss of her hair, the brunette was gone.

His attention wandered to the family of four who approached him. He shifted against the tree and swallowed the lump in his throat. Could he handle this? Reading a letter was one thing. Making the phone call another. But was he ready to look into the eyes of the recipient of Jeremy's heart?

It was too late to change his mind. The moment had arrived. Ruth wasn't with him, but he felt God's comforting presence cloak him.

"Hi, Mr. Barton, I'm Dale Smith. This is my wife Angela and son Benjamin."

"Pleased to meet you all." Noah shook hands with the portly man with the balding head, and the tall, thin woman. Then he shook the boy's hand but his attention shot back to the girl.

"And my daughter, Jessica." Dale's voice held a trace of pride.

"Hi, Jessica." Taking her hand in his, he experienced the strong, steady shake, not unlike the vise grip his son used to tease him with to make sure he felt his handshake. Noah blinked and crouched to be at eye level with the girl.

Tears crested the little girl's pale eyelashes.

Don't cry. Please don't cry.

No such luck. A tear as pure as the water that baptized Jeremy slid down her smooth, rosy cheek.

"I just want to thank you for giving me your son's heart. Now I can attend a normal school and do most of the things other girls my age do."

"That's wonderful." Though Noah had no idea what things she meant, someday he hoped to find out if he was blessed with another child. "So what are your favorite subjects?"

"Art and music, though I'm a science whiz like my dad. My mom thinks I should be a doctor or something, but I want to be a musician."

Noah's lips creased into a smile. "Being a musician would be cool, but being a doctor or a nurse and saving lives would be cool, too. There's some medical staff you should meet today. If my friend shows up, I'll have to introduce you to her."

A distant memory surfaced at the thought of careers. His son had always told him he wanted to help people and save lives. Noah stared at the light dusting of freckles on the girl's nose and cheeks. Jeremy hadn't had to grow up to do that. He'd helped in his death. "Jeremy wanted to be a fireman."

A strange expression crossed Jessica's face. "Did your son like to eat Rocky Road ice cream and chocolate?"

Noah stilled, willing the gnawing sensation in his stomach to go away. "Those were his favorites. Why?"

"It's really weird. I used to just like cupcakes and cookies, but after I got my new heart, I can't stop eating Rocky Road. Now I know why. Thanks." She threw her arms around his neck.

Bewildered and stunned at the contact, Noah looked at the girl's parents. They didn't seem to mind their daughter's hug. Should he do it? Could he hug her back?

Hesitation gripped him.

He should. He shouldn't.

He should.

As he did, he felt the steady thump of Jeremy's heart beating inside Jessica.

A tear slipped down his cheek. A piece of Jeremy still lived.

He squeezed Jessica's hands and rose to his feet. "Thank you for taking such good care of my son's heart for me."

Noah stared down into the crystal-blue eyes of Jessica Smith and swore he saw a tiny speck of Jeremy staring back at him.

God was good.

Chapter Fourteen

A little late, Ruth pulled her rental car into the nearly full parking lot of the park. Tall palm trees lining the sidewalk swayed in the slight breeze. Newly mown green grass beckoned. So did the smell of grilling meat. She couldn't wait to see the joy on the faces of the recipients and their families, and also those of the donors. This picnic was their day. A way to say thank you for their generosity.

Ruth squeezed her car between two white pickups, neither of them Noah's. Pain radiated from her heart. She'd wondered if Noah would be here today, but it looked like he wasn't and that seemed apropos for all the relationships in her life.

Although if she thought long and hard about it, she realized the feelings had pretty much been one-sided. Clutching the strap of her purse, she extricated herself from her car and followed a family of five walking toward the entrance.

The banner strung between two light poles thrummed in the slight breeze: Welcome Families. Ruth inhaled a steadying breath and walked beneath the sign.

"Hi, Ruth. Nice day today, isn't it?" One of the office staff greeted her from behind the check-in table stationed underneath a pop-up tent.

"It sure is, Tonya." Ruth signed the register and found her name badge in the stack of F's while Tonya turned to help a couple with a question.

At the beverage table stationed near the barbecue grills, a strange awareness started at the base of her neck and traveled to her hairline. There was only one person she knew that had such an affect on her. Too bad their friendship had dried up like spilt water on cement in July. Grabbing a cup of lemonade, Ruth downed the contents and crushed the cup before throwing it in the garbage can. Impossible. Noah had decided to come?

Her heart gladdened at the thought that he must have been able to meet some of the recipients after all. But he'd come alone like he'd said he would that day at his condo. Disappointment suffocated her budding happiness. Still, Noah had every right to be here just as she did. Even after the way they'd parted in the hospital, they could be cordial if they ran into each other.

Time to grab something to eat and then lose herself in a conversation with someone who cared. Turning, she collided with a rock hard chest. Noah. For the space of a heartbeat, she leaned her head against him and imagined herself wrapping her arms around his waist. They fit so well together, both inside and outside the aircraft. Yet Noah refused to take the chance.

Ruth stepped back from the contact, needing to free herself from Noah's space. She couldn't think clearly in his presence. "Oh, excuse me. I'm so sorry."

"No. I'm sorry."

An uneasy silence hung in the barbecue-scented air.

Ruth stared at the smattering of dark, curly hair protruding from the V of his sand-colored polo shirt. But that wasn't what caused her eyes to widen beneath her sunglasses or her heart to beat a little quicker. For a moment, she'd thought she'd heard him thank God for finding her here.

"Ruth. I'm glad I ran into you. Literally." He picked up her hand and held it in his, the gentle pressure warm and reassuring. Her emotions careened like an out of control car. Noah wasn't acting like the same person who'd left her at the hospital. "How are you feeling today?"

Ruth stared the man she'd fallen in love with. Her heart ached because he didn't love her in return. Instead of reaching out and caressing away the fatigue and unhappiness etched in his expression, she pulled her hand from his and forced it to her side.

Finally she found her voice. "Fine, thank you. How about you?"

"Better now."

Ruth's heartbeat accelerated until she thought it would bruise her skin. His fingers traced the delicate veins on the back of her hand before he turned it over and brought her palm to his lips. Noah's actions confused her. "Noah, why are you here?"

"I came to meet someone."

His words dashed any hope that had crept into her heart. He hadn't said he'd come to meet her. No. He'd come to meet someone else. He'd made his feelings clear at the hospital when he'd walked away without looking back. Why had she come today? Ruth mentally kicked herself. She'd fallen in love and chosen unwisely again, but this time she didn't know if her heart could take the rejection.

"Did you find them?"

"Yes. And I'd like you to meet her. She's right over

there." Noah placed his hand on the small of Ruth's back and guided her across the freshly mown grass. His hesitant grin expanded as he led her over to a small group of people standing near the food line.

"Ruth, this is Jessica Smith and her family. Jessica received Jeremy's heart. Jessica, this is Ruth Fontaine, the person I wanted you to meet earlier. Ruth is just one of the many people who make all the organ donations possible. I'm also doing my part by flying the medical teams around to retrieve them."

"I'm glad to meet you." Ruth shook the little girl's hand first and then her parents' and brother's. She loved looking into the eyes of a recipient and seeing God's work done on Earth.

Out of the corner of her eye, Ruth caught Noah's expression. At the look of pride and acceptance stamped in Noah's features, she realized that meeting with Jessica had given him the final closure on his son's death. Satisfaction filled her, even though she wished things could have ended differently between them.

Her BlackBerry rang. "Excuse me a second, please."

She stared at the number on the screen and her heartbeat accelerated. Great. Just what she needed right now, but as she'd told Noah at an earlier time, her job only knew opportunities. This was her life, her work, God's will for her. "Ruth Fontaine."

Giving a small wave to the departing family, Ruth's stomach flopped worse than if they'd just flown through an air pocket. She inhaled sharply and adjusted the phone against her ear to make sure she'd heard the person on the other end correctly. The tremor that started at her feet rioted through her body, and she caught her bottom lip between her teeth to keep the gasp inside. "Can you repeat that, please? I didn't quite catch the name of the recipient."

She stared up at Noah's questioning expression and longed to ease the uncertainty creeping into his features. A tentative smile crept over her lips.

"Thanks, Lou. Tell the driver I'll meet him and the team at Phoenix Memorial. I'll be there in fifteen minutes." Disconnecting the call, Ruth flipped her hair behind her shoulders.

"It's Marissa's heart, isn't it?"

Ruth shook her head.

"Tommy's?"

"No." Ruth shook her head again, though she wished she were going on recoveries for her kids as well. Still, happiness radiated from inside. This was the first recovery she'd go on where she actually knew someone close to the recipient. "But it's someone you know."

"Hannah?" Hope and relief radiated from Noah's expression. "A kidney's become available?" He whooped, wrapped his arms around Ruth's waist, picked her up and then twirled her around. Instinctively, Ruth wrapped her arms around Noah's neck and held on, his giddiness contagious, and she found herself laughing along with him.

"Yes. Apparently so. Now if you'll put me down, I can go get it for her."

Her feet back on the ground, yet still a little dizzy, Ruth maintained her grip around Noah's neck. She gasped for breath. The instant surge of energy at the contact made her knees buckle and her heart race. Especially when she felt the weight of Noah's gaze. His excitement held more than a promise for what could come if he'd allow himself to love again.

"Come on. Let's go. I'm coming with you."

"Really?"

"Really. I want to be a part of it."

"Oh, Noah." Moisture crested on her lashes. *Don't you dare cry, Ruth Fontaine.* Too late. A tear rolled down her cheek, followed by another. For a heartbeat that seemed to stretch into the next minute, Ruth stared in Noah's sunglasses, almost not recognizing the grinning reflection staring back at her. "Then what are we waiting for?"

"Nothing." His gentle fingers wiped away her tears before he locked his hand over hers and headed toward the parking lot. "But why are you meeting a driver? Where's the kidney?"

"Casa Grande. AeroFlight has a van that will take the team and I down to recover the kidney and then bring us back."

"Why not take a plane?" Noah matched her step for step as they strode across the grass, bypassing several families waiting at the check-in table.

"Because kidneys can remain outside the body longer so there's no need to add the extra expense of an airplane." Ruth acknowledged her boss's wave and mimicked a phone call. The white-haired man nodded and gave her a two-fingered salute.

"But what if I insist. I can fly everyone to and from Casa Grande before the van would even get there. Then Hannah would have her kidney that much sooner."

Ruth slowed and turned toward him before she stepped onto the pavement. "You'd do that for Hannah?"

Noah tucked an errant strand of hair behind her ear and let his thumb trace a line along her jaw and over her chin to rest against her lips. "Yes. I'd do it for Marissa or Tommy or any one of the children if you asked me to. And I'd do it for you. You're not afraid. Are you?"

Ruth shook her head and grinned up at him. "Not with you as the pilot."

"I'll call Brad. You get the team to the airport."

Regret and anticipation cohabited inside Ruth when Noah ended the contact, yet she grinned at him as she pulled out her phone. "You are something else."

Once Noah's Citation came to a stop on the tarmac in Scottsdale, he stared at the cooler by the Ruth's feet. He wondered what the kidney looked like. A chicken liver, only bigger? Red or brown or some sort of pink? Did it pulse on its own without signals from the brain? Or did it just lie there, waiting.

Someday he'd have to ask Ruth.

Wonderful things did happen, and he'd been a part of making this one take place. But he was certain God had played a larger role—not only in this, but in bringing Ruth into his life. *Thank you, Lord.*

He secured the plane and opened the door for the surgical team to unload and walk toward the waiting ambulance. With her job mainly completed, Ruth stayed behind, finishing up her paperwork. Beside him, Brad hovered like a lost puppy.

"Why don't you follow them to the hospital? I'll finish up here."

"Thanks, Noah." Brad ran down the steps and sweet-talked his way inside the vehicle.

"Hang on, Ruth. I'll be done in a second."

Ruth looked up and gave him one of her sunny smiles that melted the last remnants of any resistance. "No problem. I'm almost done myself. Besides, since you drove, I don't have much of a choice, do I?"

"No, I suppose you don't. I'm hungry. How about you?

Let's go grab something to eat. I know a great little Italian place you'd like, and then we can take in a movie."

Ruth hooked her arm through his and rested her head against his shoulder. "Sounds like a plan. I hope you like romantic comedies because I've wanted to see that new movie that's been getting such rave reviews."

"I'm game."

Hours later Noah stood outside Ruth's front door, the entryway well lit by the motion lights he'd installed. When Ruth stifled a yawn, Noah knew he should leave, yet he didn't want the night to end.

He loved Ruth. Pure and simple.

He wanted her in his life to share the triumphs and the disappointments. To wake up next to her in the mornings and hold her until the sleep disappeared from her eyes. To come back from a flight and have her in their home with waffles on the table and a little boy or girl waiting to wrap his or her chubby arms around his legs.

He wanted a do-over with Ruth. He wanted another relationship. He'd rather love Ruth and take the chance on losing her again than remain alone for the rest of his life. She fit so well with him. He hoped he could convince her they had a future together.

Nervous as a truant student, he shifted on his feet. The next few minutes would change the course of his life in a way he couldn't have imagined a few weeks ago. Rivulets of sweat formed on his brow. "May I come in for some coffee?"

"Sure. It'll only take a few minutes to make." Ruth unlocked the front door and stepped inside.

Noah followed behind Ruth and barely made it down the hallway before his cell phone rang and broke the stillness. After eyeing the number on the screen, he warily flipped the phone open. They'd barely brought Hannah's kidney back four hours ago. Had something gone wrong? "Hi, Brad. How's Hannah?"

Tangible relief flooded him at his partner's words. After disconnecting, Noah shoved the phone back into his pocket and grabbed Ruth around the waist. Her hands gripped his forearms as he swung her around the kitchen. Her surprised laughter joined his. "What happened?"

"The surgery was a success, and Hannah's fine. Thank you, Ruth. We make a good team, don't we?"

Ruth's laughter died, and her expression grew serious, leaving him wondering if he'd done something else wrong. Another bead of sweat rolled down his cheek. Had he made an error in judgment?

"Yes, we do." She wrapped her arms around his neck, and in that instant he knew everything would be all right.

When she gazed up at him, he thought of warm summer nights and fresh baked cookies. He could never grow tired of being near her. The kitchen light reflected the gold in Ruth's hair but her true riches lay deep inside. She'd been brought into his life because he'd needed her to guide him back into the light. He looked out the window at the midnight-blue sky, and more peace settled around his shoulders.

"Does this mean what I think it means?" A smile hugged her lips.

Noah set her back down in the floor and rubbed her back. "It does. I love you, Ruth. You've shown me how to live again and brought me back to God. The past few days apart have been awful. I want to spend the rest of my life with you."

Ruth stilled and tilted her head to look up at him. Her

green eyes widened as a sob caught in her throat. His fingers traced the contours of her cheeks. Then Noah dipped his head and slanted his lips over hers. Forget about words right now. He didn't need them to communicate what his heart felt. His actions would do more.

Moments later, Noah lifted his head. When Ruth saw the love shining from his eyes, she had the answer she needed and quit hiding behind excuses. Noah would never forget about his first wife or his son, just as she would never forget her twin sister; yet both of them had finally managed to put the past behind them and find the love God had meant for them in the process.

"I love you, too, Noah. I want that too. You don't think Houston will mind, do you?"

"I know he won't." Noah leaned down and kissed her again.

* * * * *

Dear Reader,

Welcome to my first book for Steeple Hill. I'm thrilled to be a part of the Harlequin family. I loved writing *On Wings of Love* because it gave me a chance to explore the challenging and complex issue of organ donation and I learned so much during my research. The recipient and donor family stories I read, as well as having a personal experience on the recipient side, were truly inspiring and humbling at the same time.

On Wings of Love is very near and dear to my heart because my sister-in-law, Susan, to whom this book is dedicated, is a kidney and liver recipient. Through the grace of God and the generosity of an organ donor, she's alive today and welcomed her first grandbaby into the world just over a year ago.

While Ruth and Noah are fictitious, their issues and past experiences are something that we can identify with. In our daily lives we are faced with numerous obstacles, setbacks and sometimes life-changing decisions, but our faith helps us through these difficult times. As Noah rediscovered, God is good.

I love to hear from my readers about how my books have touched their lives. Please visit my Web site at www.kimwatters.com or my group blog www.muchcheaperthantherapy.blogspot.com. You may also write me c/o Steeple Hill Books, 233 Broadway, Suite 1001, New York, NY. 10279.

Blessings,
Kim Watters

QUESTIONS FOR DISCUSSION

1. In *On Wings of Love*, Ruth's first introduction to Noah is when she overhears the fight between the two pilots chartered to fly her and her medical team to San Diego. Can you think of a better way Noah might have handled the situation? How would you have handled it?

2. Helping people is what Ruth does best. What are some of the things Ruth does to help others? What are some of the things you can do to help others?

3. Noah turned his back on God after the death of his wife and son. Has there ever been a circumstance in your life where you question His intentions? What did you do? How did you resolve your conflict?

4. Why do you think God allows such difficult things to happen to His children?

5. In grieving over his son, Noah feels that he should have been able to do something to save Jeremy instead of signing his organs over for donation. Guilt is a powerful emotion and shut down Noah's ability to move forward. What are some other things guilt can do? How can faith help overcome that feeling? How can we help others who are facing grief?

6. Ruth believes she's doing God's will on earth. What are some things you can do that serve God?

7. What is Noah's reaction when he discovers his office manager needs a kidney transplant to lead a more normal life? Why does he delay in going to Ruth for help? What would you do if you faced a similar circumstance?

8. When Noah drives Ruth to the funeral for her friend, he feels uncomfortable with the group of mourners, especially when the minister invites him to join in. Why? Have you ever felt afraid or scared of a new situation? How did you handle it?

9. Both Ruth and Noah are scarred by what happened to them in the past. How did it affect their lives and career choices? Have you ever had something happen to you in the past that affected the choices you've made? How did you handle them?

10. When Noah sees Hannah and Dylan at the park, it brings back happy memories of his son and his anger and bitterness start to recede. What special things do you do together as a family? What traditions have you carried on or new traditions have you started? What traditions would you like to start?

11. Noah and Ruth are determined to be friends. Friends care for and help each other during the good times and the bad like Ruth is there for Noah when he needs her. Think about all the friends that have come and gone in your life when you needed them. Is there anyone you've lost touch with that meant a lot to you? What's keeping you from reaching out to renew your friendship?

12. When Noah sees all the sick children at the hospital, he wonders how God can turn his back on them, especially the boy he befriends. He soon discovers perhaps the hospital is where the children are supposed to be taken care of. Illness can create a lot of stress in the family. Have you faced this challenge? How did your faith help you through it?

13. When Ruth loses her first donor and suffers a few more setbacks, she is ready to quit her job. Has there ever been a time when you've had enough with your job? What decision did you make? Did it make you happy? Would you make the same decision today?

14. When Noah visits Ruth in the hospital after the plane crash, he's paralyzed with fear and guilt at losing Ruth like he lost his first wife. His attempt to shut off his emotions stall though when he realizes that by denying his love for her, he is denying himself happiness and rejecting what God has intended. Has there ever been a time when you rejected what God had intended for you? What happened? How did you make your peace with God?

15. When Noah meets the recipient of his son's heart, he's finally able to let go and embrace life again. He realizes his son saved lives that day and through the grace of God, Jeremy still lives. So when he learns that a kidney has become available for Hannah, he jumps at the chance to help bring the organ back for her. Have you ever changed your opinion about something? How did you feel about it?

Read on for a sneak preview of
KATIE'S REDEMPTION
by Patricia Davids,
the first book in the heartwarming new
BRIDES OF AMISH COUNTRY *series*
available in March 2010
from Steeple Hill Love Inspired.

When a pregnant formerly Amish woman
returns to her brother's house, seeking forgiveness
and a place to give birth to her child,
what she finds there isn't what she expected.

*P*lease, God, don't let them send me away.

To give her child a home Katie Lantz would endure the angry tirade she expected from her brother. Through it all Malachi wouldn't be able to hide the gloating in his voice.

An unexpected tightening across her stomach made Katie suck in a quick breath. She'd been up since dawn, riding for hours on the jolting bus.

Her stomach tightened again. The pain deepened. Something wasn't right. This was more than fatigue. It was labor.

Breathing hard, she peered through the blowing snow. It wasn't much farther to her brother's farm. Closing her eyes, she gathered her strength.

One foot in front of the other. The only way to finish a journey is to start it.

She sagged with relief when her hand closed over the railing. She was home.

Home. The word echoed inside her mind, bringing with it unhappy memories that pushed aside her relief. Raising her fist, she knocked at the front door. Then she bowed her head and closed her eyes, grasping the collar of her coat to keep the chill at bay.

When the door finally opened, she looked up to meet her brother's gaze.

Katie sucked in a breath and then took a half step back. A tall, broad-shouldered Amish man stood in front of her with a kerosene lamp in his hand and a faintly puzzled expression on his handsome face.

It wasn't Malachi.

To read more of Katie's story,
pick up KATIE'S REDEMPTION
by Patricia Davids, available March 2010.

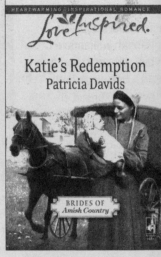

LARGER-PRINT BOOKS

Love Inspired

2 NEW STORIES IN 1 BOOK

From two bestselling authors comes this volume
containing two heartwarming Easter stories that
celebrate the renewal of love, life and faith.

Easter Promises
by
Lois Richer and Allie Pleiter

Available March wherever books are sold.